BAT

Stephen Thraves

Illustrated by Terry Oakes

HODDER AND STOUGHTON
LONDON SYDNEY AUCKLAND

British Library Cataloguing in Publication Data

A catalogue record for this book
is available from the British Library

ISBN 0 340 56600 0

Published by Hodder and Stoughton Children's Books,
a division of Hodder and Stoughton Ltd,
Mill Road, Dunton Green, Sevenoaks, Kent TN13 2YA

Photoset by Rowland Phototypesetting Ltd,
Bury St Edmunds, Suffolk

Printed and bound in Great Britain by
BPCC Hazells Ltd
Member of BPCC Ltd

Welcome, fearless one! You have entered the shadowy mythical world of BATTLE QUEST. It is a world of magic and hideous monsters, of treasure and deadly conflict. It is a world where only the most strong, skilful and daring survive. All others perish, forgotten, in its gloom.

Are YOU strong, skilful and daring enough? You will assume the body, mind and courage of a barbarian hero but the dangers that await you will test even your famed abilities to the full. You will have to fight monster warriors of incredible strength; outwit wizards and goblins of exceptional cunning. Tests, traps and deceits lie at every turn. The decisions you make will be gambling with your very life!

Everything you need for your perilous quest is contained within the special wallet. There is one rotating counter to record your increasing or diminishing strength, and another to record how many treasures you have found. There are also various *spell, special powers* and *equipment* cards that are waiting to be picked up at various points in the adventure, and two coloured dice for when battles have to be fought.

Unless you are very lucky, it is unlikely that you will succeed on your very first adventure. You will find that the more times you play, the more skilful you become in making the right decisions and taking the right risks. Your skill-level is represented by the number of treasures you record on the treasure counter and you should aim to keep improving this score until you reach the maximum of *8 treasures*. Only then are you worthy of your great fame!

BACKGROUND

'**Y**our voyage was safe, I trust?' a man in purple robes says, greeting you as you step from the small galley that carried you all these miles. 'I am Uvane, Queen Tarsha's Chief Adviser. I know your journey was long, but Queen Tarsha requests your presence at her castle immediately. That is how urgent our plight is. Please step into my chariot.'

The chariot's four horses convey you both at breakneck speed, Uvane's servant liberal with the whip. You are soon approaching the drawbridge of the royal castle. 'Open, fools!' Uvane yells at the drawbridge guards. 'My guest is to see our Queen without delay!'

Surrounded by her officials, Queen Tarsha is waiting for you on the other side of the drawbridge, in the castle's large courtyard. She is sitting on a stone throne which is strewn with the skins of wild animals. She rises as you approach.

'Can you save us, Barbarian hero?' she asks in an imperial voice as you go down on bended knee before her. 'Can you save our once prosperous and happy kingdom? You are our last hope!'

The legend that reached your country was true: Queen Tarsha has a beauty that knows no equal. But you respectfully keep your eyes lowered, holding yourself too humble to admire that beauty further.

'You perhaps don't believe, Barbarian, that this was once a very prosperous land?' her aloof voice continues. 'You doubtless witnessed all the beggars on your short ride through my kingdom, all the disease that now afflicts my people. You doubtless noticed that the robes of my courtiers here look threadbare and ragged. But I assure you that not long ago we were a kingdom of immense wealth, provided by the large diamond mine in the north of my land; probably the richest source of diamonds ever discovered!'

So that was another legend about this land that was founded on truth. But she was right. You *had* found this rumour of great wealth very hard to believe during your journey from harbour to castle. All you could see from the Chief Adviser's chariot was poverty and neglect.

'You must be intrigued to know the cause of this sudden reversal of fortune,' she says, her voice starting to lose some of its regal composure. Anger is creeping in, bitterness. 'Draxun – *he* was the cause! He is ruler of the kingdom just beyond the diamond mine, on the other side of the mountains there. His envious eyes have long looked towards our prosperous lands. Some years back he asked for my hand in marriage. But I knew the real purpose in his proposal, of course. It was not my heart he wanted by the alliance, but my diamond mine!

'When I refused him,' she continues, 'he swore devastating revenge on me and my kingdom. Not only was his greed thwarted but his pride was stung as well!'

Eyes still to the ground, you wait to hear the nature of this revenge but it's a while before Queen Tarsha can go on. It's as if she won't speak until she can remove the emotion from her voice, until she can restore the regal dignity.

'With threat of public and gruesome execution,' she explains coldly and matter-of-factly, 'Draxun ordered his Chief Sorcerer, Murgle, to cast a hideous spell on the diamond mine. He was to fill it with vicious demons and monsters so that my miners would be too terrified to work it any more. Needless to say, the cowardly sorcerer obeyed his master's instruction. Every twist and tunnel of the mine now echoes with one of his monstrous creations.

'So we still have the diamonds there,' she concludes, 'but no one brave enough to mine them. My kingdom therefore no longer has anything to trade with for food and clothing. My people go half-naked, they starve. That is the curse Murgle has put on us, that is how Draxun has wreaked his evil revenge!'

You next feel the touch of her hand on your shoulder. She orders you to rise.

'I say again,' she states, allowing you to look directly at her, 'YOU are our last hope. I ask you to go down into the mine yourself and rescue those diamonds – as many as you can. If you agree, I and my people will be eternally indebted to you. If you refuse – or your quest fails – my kingdom is surely doomed!'

How will you eventually decide? Will you agree to embark on this awesome quest or not? If you do, turn the page . . .

QUEST INSTRUCTIONS

Your strength

1. Before starting your quest at paragraph 1 overleaf, it is necessary to record your starting *strength* on your STRENGTH COUNTER. Your starting strength is six, so turn the counter until **6** shows through the window. Every time you are weakened in some way during the adventure, you must change this number to the next one down. When you reach **0** you are dead and must immediately stop your quest. If you wish to make another attempt at it, you must start the game all over again.

2. There are three ways you can be weakened during the quest. First, as a result of foolishness on your part (drinking a poisonous potion, for example); second, because of strenuous activity; or third, because you have been wounded in battle.

Fighting battles

3. A battle is fought by simultaneous throwing of the two special dice. The blue dice is YOU, the barbarian hero armed with *sword* and *shield*. The red dice represents your various monster adversaries: the 'fanged head' representing the *monster* and the scimitar representing its *weapon* or – if it doesn't carry a weapon – its slashing claw or tail.

4. You keep simultaneously throwing the two dice until either you or your monster adversary inflicts a wound. For a wound to be inflicted, one dice must show a weapon uppermost while the other must show the opponent unprotected. Thus, if the blue dice shows the sword and the red dice the monster, then *you* have wounded the *monster*. But if the blue dice shows the barbarian and the red dice the scimitar then the *monster* has wounded *you*.

5. Any other combination of the dice (see table overleaf) means that a wound hasn't been inflicted on either side and so you must continue throwing the dice until one has.

6. When a *monster* is wounded, make a mental note of this and then resume the dice-throwing. This is because a monster will always

fight to the death and you only slay it completely if you are able to inflict a certain number of wounds. That number will vary with each monster and part of the skill of the game is to try to find the monsters that are the least resilient. (So don't be too eager to fight each monster you encounter. You don't have to challenge *every* monster to succeed at the game and others, possibly weaker ones, will often be encountered very soon afterwards.)

7. If *you* are wounded at any point during the battle, however, you must always prudently take flight at once. Thus, you immediately stop the dice-throwing.

𝕸agic spells, 𝕾pecial powers, 𝕰quipment

8. Because the world of BATTLE QUEST is a magical as well as violent one, there are various magic spells and special powers to be gained during your adventures. There are also useful items of equipment to be found. These accessories vary from adventure to adventure but the ones accompanying this particular BATTLE QUEST adventure are: a TRANCE SPELL, FORESIGHT POWER, a CRYPTICS SCROLL, and the BOOK OF CIPHERS. Possession of these cards will greatly improve the chances of succeeding in your quest and you should therefore make very effort to locate them during the adventure. But until you do locate them, you must keep these four cards face down and out of play.

𝕿reasure counter

9. The object of the quest is not only to come out of it alive but also to collect as much treasure as possible. You record all treasure collected on the TREASURE COUNTER. Set this at **0** to start with and then try and attain as high a score as possible during the quest. The more times you attempt the quest, the better your score should be. When you have obtained the maximum score of eight treasures, then you have indeed completely mastered THE TUNNELS OF FEAR!

DICE TABLE

RED   BLUE

  Monster momentarily
exposed and you wound it
with your *sword*

  Monster's weapon wounds *you*

  Weapons clash (i.e. no
advantage to either side)

  Monster strikes but you
defend against this with
your *shield*

  Monster momentarily exposed
but only your *shield* is to the
fore so you're unable to take
advantage

  Both *monster* and *you* are
momentarily exposed but
neither side able to take
advantage

$\mathfrak{Y}$OU ARE NOW READY TO START. $\mathfrak{I}$ WISH
YOU EVERY LUCK IN YOUR QUEST
AND DEARLY HOPE THAT THE GODS
ARE ON YOUR SIDE . . .

'Come! It is time for us to go,' Uvane tells you after you have been allowed a few hours rest in the castle. He lets you quickly finish your goblet of mead before escorting you back to his chariot. 'I will transport you to within a few miles of the diamond mine,' he says as his servant cracks his whip over a fresh team of horses, 'but the very last part of the journey you must make on foot. It's there that the mountains start to rise and the terrain is treacherous.' As the horses snort and pound in front of you, their flowing white manes sleek in the wind, you again observe all the poverty and decay that has taken over this land. There's mile upon mile of this depressing sight but, at last – after some three hours in the chariot – the grey-blue silhouette of the mountains starts slowly to rise on the horizon. Uvane stops his chariot much sooner than you were expecting – for although the rough road now begins to climb, the climb is still gentle. It makes you wonder whether the Chief Adviser has another reason for not wishing to take you any further: fear. 'You will find the entrance to the mine about an hour's walk from here,' he tells you, then quickly orders his chariot to be turned round. 'Good luck. I hope for both our sakes that you succeed!' As you are left alone there on the mountain road, you wonder whether you should start your walk towards the mine immediately or rest a while after your long, uncomfortable journey.

If you prefer to set off immediately	**go to 127**
If you prefer to rest	**go to 203**

2
THIS CREATURE
IS SLAIN BY

WOUNDS

Wage combat by simultaneously throwing the two dice. If you slay the creature, go to 43. If the creature inflicts a wound on you first, deduct 1 from your STRENGTH RATING and then flee well away from this cavern by hurrying to 289.

3

You cautiously climb into the crater, slowly making your way down its steeply-sloping side. Fortunately there are enough ledges and crevices there to provide a series of hand and foot holds; but you wonder how long this will continue. Right to the very depths of the crater? Quite soon, though, your foot suddenly touches the bottom. *Go to 287.*

4

The tunnel seems to grow ever larger as you progress, it must now be a good fifteen metres high. As you are looking up at the shadowy roof, you suddenly notice a small cave just below it, recessed into the top of the tunnel wall. If it was *just* the cave there, you probably wouldn't have given it a second thought; you have encountered a fair number of these high-up recesses already. But what is intriguing is that there are three ropes dangling from the hole. It would seem that this particular cave is actually *used* in some way. Could it be as a storage place for some of the mined diamonds? you wonder. You immediately approach the three ropes so you can climb one of them. Which will you choose?

If rope on left	**go to 217**
If rope in centre	**go to 182**
If rope on right	**go to 46**
If decide it wiser not to climb	**go to 33**

5

You forge deeper and deeper into the mountain, the trail of lamps twisting dimly in front of you. Suddenly, however, you stop. The next section of the tunnel looks unstable, its creaking roof showering occasional falls of dust and rock fragments. Each shower becomes slightly thicker, heavier, piling its dust and stones on the tunnel floor. Just in case this suddenly develops into a rock-fall, you wonder whether you should stay where you are for a while. But maybe even where you are isn't completely safe, and you would do better to try and quickly pass through this section of the tunnel.

If you have acquired FORESIGHT POWER during your adventure, you may employ it here to find out whether it's best to

wait or continue. To do this, place the FORESIGHT POWER
CARD exactly over the eye shape below. If you haven't acquired
FORESIGHT POWER, you'll have to hope for the best in
making your decision.

If you decide to wait   **go to 204**
If you decide to continue   **go to 133**

6

You start to climb down the series of rungs you have chosen, careful
not to lose your footing. The long echoes in the shaft suggest that it
is very deep and a fall would almost certainly be the end of you.
Your task is not an easy one for there are no lamps on your way
down. You only hope that they will begin again as soon as you reach
the base. At last, you seem to be nearing the ground. Suddenly,
however, one of the rungs gives way under your foot and you fall.
Although you weren't that high up, you still receive a severe jar to
your spine. This injury is bound to handicap you a little in your
quest.

Deduct 1 from your STRENGTH RATING. Go next to 91.

7

The creature howls in agony, the single eye filling with even more
red veins as it staggers from your last sword-thrust. The bloodshot

eye grows more and more bulbous and you're sure it's about to explode. But a leathery eyelid slowly draws across it as the creature slumps to the ground. It will open no more. You step over the expired creature, plucking your prize from the heap of fallen rocks. You immediately drop the diamond into your haversack so you can press on with your exploration of the mine.

Add 1 to the score on your TREASURE COUNTER. Now hurry well away from this cavern by going to 289.

8

You take the woollen robe from the sorcerer, inserting your arms into the sleeves and loosely knotting the tasselled rope at its waist. But as you reach back to draw its deep hood over you, the sorcerer suddenly shakes his head. 'I'm afraid you chose wrongly, my friend,' he tells you. 'You would only have learnt the secret of one of my spells if you had chosen the silk robe.' You quickly divest yourself of the robe you are wearing so you can replace it with the silk one. But as you reach out to take it from the sorcerer's arm, both it and the sorcerer vanish into thin air. *Go to 99.*

9

Still slowly beckoning her finger at you from over her shoulder, the green-gowned form leads you towards the left side of the cavern. She makes you walk as close to this side as possible and this convinces you that you made the correct choice between the three spirits. As close to the tunnel wall as this, you should be able to avoid both rock-falls from above and unseen potholes below. But then you notice a strange sticky slime on your left shoulder. In fact it's all over your left side – on your forearm, your hand, your thigh. Suddenly, your body starts to feel weak, your eyesight starts to blur. It seems as if this sticky slime is sucking all the strength out of you. A moment or two later, you collapse to the ground . . .

Deduct 1 from your STRENGTH RATING. Go next to 224.

10

You were right. The creature _wouldn't_ stray from its position to stop you passing it. It certainly snarls and hisses at you, fiercely taunting you for your lack of courage, but it remains where it is. The sorcerer Murgle obviously threatened death to any creature that deserted its precious charge. This again seems to be confirmed by sight of the next fiend you encounter, some hundred metres or so further along the tunnel. As ferociously as the fanged creature rages and taunts, impatiently brandishing a scimitar at you, it stays very close to the

diamond it guards. It's almost as if it has been chained there – although there are no irons evident on the creature's hooved feet. Its dread of Murgle is obviously 'irons' enough.

If you wish to fight creature	**go to 122**
If you wish to avoid it	**go to 181**

11

The bread seems perfectly all right. In fact, it's quite delicious. The loaf is still warm and it has a rich yeasty smell. As you hungrily tear off one chunk after another, you wonder for whom the bread was intended. You assume it was for the monsters. Perhaps it was left here to cool down before a goblin took it round to the fiends. But then with horror you realise that the bread had a very different purpose. It *was* a trap after all. For you suddenly start to choke, clutching your throat. As your body grows weak, you only hope that you didn't eat enough of the bread for its poison to be fatal . . .

Deduct 1 from your STRENGTH RATING. Go next to 52.

12

The ravine finally starts to narrow, the wall of fire squeezed thinner and thinner. Eventually both it and the ravine peter out. The two halves of the tunnel floor have joined together again. So your path is once more very wide, but it's not long before this cavern-like tunnel splits up into three smaller ones. There are lamps in all three of the twisting branches, so one seems as good as the other. Which will you decide to enter?

If left branch   **go to 177**
If middle branch   **go to 228**
If right branch   **go to 84**

It seems that your choice of pool was a good one because you wade through it without injury. All your fears were unjustified. The pool isn't deceptively deep and nor does it suddenly turn into a scalding fury. As you step out of the pool, however, you start to feel rather strange. It's as if all the strength has been sucked out of you. The pool obviously *wasn't* so harmless after all. As you stagger forwards, you can only hope that the water's evil effect is just temporary . . .

Deduct 1 from your STRENGTH RATING. Go next to 112.

14

A cold shiver runs down your spine as the skull softly and eerily addresses you. 'I can restore the strength you have lost in the fall,' it speaks through yellowed jaws. 'You merely have to put out your hand and touch me.' This you start to do, extending your arm towards the skull. But then you suddenly yank your arm back again, wondering whether this is another trap. Perhaps making contact with that ghostly apparition will weaken you even further . . .

If you have been taught the TRANCE SPELL during your adventure, you may cast it here to hypnotise the skull into telling you whether it's lying or not. To do this, place the TRANCE

SPELL CARD exactly over the skull's 'mind square' below. If you haven't been taught the TRANCE SPELL, you'll have to hope for the best in deciding what to do.

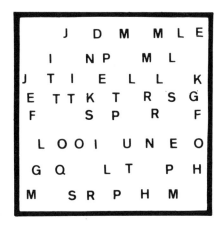

```
      J   D   M     M   L   E

   I     N P     M   L

J   T   I   E   L   L       K
  E  T T  K  T   R  S  G
  F      S  P   R      F

   L  O  I    U  N  E   O

   G  Q     L  T    P   H

 M     S  R  P  H  M
```

If you decide to touch skull	**go to 64**
If you decide to ignore it	**go to 111**

15

Mercifully, the excruciating wail at last subsides. With the hideous sound still ringing in your ears, you rise slowly to your feet again. Your brain seems very groggy but at least you can just about continue with your quest. *Go to 328.*

16
THIS CREATURE
IS SLAIN BY

WOUNDS

Wage combat by simultaneously throwing the two dice. If you slay the creature, go to 316. If the creature inflicts a wound on you first, deduct 1 from your STRENGTH RATING and then flee well away from this region by hurrying to 5.

17

Groaning and whining, the creature drags its wounded body slowly towards the portcullis. It edges its way underneath. You wonder where it is heading. Just to the outside of the cave, you presume – it won't get much further. Perhaps it just wants to be free of its prison when it dies. But then you suddenly realise that it's purpose is much more sinister. It's trying to reach the portcullis's winch! It's trying to trap you inside the cave! Fortunately, however, just as it stretches out a claw towards the winch, it shudders and dies. Greatly relieved, you can now turn your attention to the sparkling diamond in the cave . . .

Add 1 to the score on your TREASURE COUNTER. Now hurry well away from this region by going to 29.

18

As you continue along the tunnel, you hear dripping in the distance. Turning a couple more bends, you see that these drips are coming from the tunnel roof. There are three series of drips, each having formed a large pool immediately beneath it. The pools are so close together that your path is completely blocked. The only way across is by wading through one of the pools . . . *Go to 215.*

19

The creature tries to gnaw its way through the thick iron portcullis with it's grotesque fanged mouth and it is so determined that you could almost believe it will succeed. The only realistic means of removing the sturdy gate, though, is by turning the winch. And

that, fortunately, is on *your* side of the portcullis. But might you decide to turn the winch yourself? For if the portcullis stops the creature getting *out* of the cave, it also stops you getting *in*. Your reason for considering entry into the cave is, of course, that magnificent diamond . . .

If you wish to fight creature   **go to 152**
If you wish to avoid it   **go to 276**

20

You cling to the jutting rocks on the right side of the tunnel, gradually making your way past the furious whirlwind. Although it lashes at your face, you're just able to resist its powerful sucking. Suddenly the whirlwind starts to move its position and your heart nearly stops. But it swirls away from you, not towards you, making your passage even less hazardous. Soon you're well past the whirlwind. *Go to 307.*

21

The goblin snarls at you as you keep your haversack firmly closed. You wonder whether this snarl will suddenly change into pleasant laughter, but it doesn't. It becomes even worse. The creature's colour also remains constant now – a furious red. You're sure he's about to advance on you and try to take the diamond by force, so you quickly draw your sword. But then something quite extraordinary happens to the goblin. He starts to dissolve. You watch stupefied as he slowly disappears. You are even more thankful now that you didn't give him the diamond. If you had, then it might have vanished with him! *Go to 197.*

22

With another cruel, manic cackle, the sorcerer suddenly brings his hand down again. Immediately there's a flash before your eyes, momentarily blinding you. When you can see again, you find that the wizard has vanished but – more strangely – three oak doors have suddenly appeared in front of you. Are they real or imaginary? The only way to find out is to step up to one of them . . .

<blockquote>

If you choose left door   **go to 315**

If you choose middle door   **go to 121**

If you choose right door   **go to 72**

</blockquote>

23

'I wish to help those who challenge Draxun and his evil sorcerer,' the wizard tells you quickly. 'I will not give my reasons for this because they would take too long and it would be very bad for me if I were to be found in these mines. It is enough for me to warn you that there is danger ahead. One of these items of clothing can protect you against this danger. Put on no more than one item, though, or you will be cursed.' Before you can ask him which one, however, the wizard has disappeared.

If you have been given the POWER OF FORESIGHT, you may employ it here to find out what this danger is (and, therefore, which item of clothing you should wear). To do this, place the POWER OF FORESIGHT CARD exactly over the 'eye' shape below. If you haven't been given the POWER OF FORE-SIGHT, you'll just have to guess which piece of clothing to wear.

If you choose boots   **go to 148**
If you choose helmet   **go to 286**
If you choose earmuffs   **go to 108**

24

You carefully let the rope feed through your hands, slowly lowering the cage. When there's only about ten metres to go, however, you glance down. A bed of long iron spikes has suddenly appeared on the ground, directly beneath your cage! You quickly start pulling the rope to make the cage rise again but it suddenly seems to have a will of its own. It's determined to hurtle downwards, straight for the spikes. *Go to 245.*

25
THIS CREATURE
IS SLAIN BY

WOUNDS

Wage combat by simultaneously throwing the two dice. If you slay the creature, go to 288. If the creature inflicts a wound on you first, deduct 1 from your STRENGTH RATING and then flee well away from this region by hurrying to 27.

26

Your weary arms drop your shield and resignedly you wait for the sword to make its fatal thrust. But it's just at that moment that the sword also drops to the ground. The evil magic abruptly seems to have left it. Certainly, its blue glow has now gone, and it lies there looking just like your trusty old friend again. You tentatively reach out towards it, to take it up and return it to its sheath. But you are ready to pull back your hand if it suddenly comes to life once more. It doesn't, though, so you happily grasp your weapon and return it to its scabbard. *Go to 197.*

27

The tunnels seem to go on and on, penetrating deeper and deeper into the bowels of the mountain. Tiredness begins to overcome you so you sit on a rock to rest for a few minutes. As you are sitting there, resting to recover your strength, a young woman appears in front of you, dressed in a long, white gown. 'I am the Guardian Spirit of this mine,' she tells you softly. 'The next section of this tunnel becomes very treacherous, so you must follow me for the safest route.' As she starts to beckon you with a slim pale finger, however, something quite incredible suddenly happens to her. Something that makes you gape in shock . . . *Go to 269.*

28

There's also the lethal, curved gleam of a scimitar; a scimitar in the clawed fist of a fanged monster. It's the most repulsive creature you've ever seen – thick hair all over its body but not so much as a strand on its head. It has only one eye in the centre of this head, an

eye as bulbous as a frog's and laced with red veins. The grotesque eye leers at you, challenging you to try and come and take the diamond.

If you wish to fight creature   **go to 100**
If you wish to avoid it   **go to 155**

29

Sometimes walking, sometimes breaking into a run, you continue down this long snaking tunnel. Finally it leads into a large cavern. There are two other tunnels emerging here and you assume these to be the other branches you could have taken. You make your way across the cavern so you can continue your journey. But you find that there *isn't* any continuation from here. The far side of the cavern is a solid wall of rock. You have obviously explored all there is to the mine. So you turn round in order to start the long journey back. You're just wondering which tunnel you should leave by when disaster strikes . . . **Go to 194.**

30

Unfortunately the potion has absolutely no effect. You feel just as dazed and racked with pain as before. The other two goblets are still there, though. You had expected them to disappear suddenly when you raised this one to your lips. So, in spite of the fact that he saved your life, you decide to disobey the spirit and try a second potion. When you reach out for the goblet in the middle, however, another rumbling starts in this part of the tunnel. You immediately leave the spot, slowly and painfully continuing in the direction Gurn instructed. **Go to 123.**

31

Lekk leads you to the far side of the cavern again. 'We must squeeze through here,' he tells you – and, to your surprise, you see that it isn't just a solid wall of rock after all. There's a deep gash behind a large upright boulder. The gash takes you through to yet another partly-lit tunnel! **Go to 208.**

32

You wonder where you are for a moment, slowly returning from your unconsciousness. You see the tunnel roof above you. You splutter a couple of times. Has something been smothering your face? But then you spit out a couple of feathers and you remember. That monstrous bird! You quickly rise to your feet, worried that it might still be lurking somewhere nearby. To your immense relief, though, it seems to have flown off or vanished into thin air. *Go to 236.*

33

You have walked quite a way from the cave when your eyes are drawn to a small ledge on the left side of the tunnel. There is a large loaf of bread sitting there! You haven't eaten for hours, having given away all the food you brought with you to the starving children you passed on your way to the mine. If you don't eat soon, it's likely to have an effect on your strength. But just as you're about to tear off a piece of the bread, you wonder if it has been put there as a trap . . . if it could be poisoned!

If you have been given the POWER OF FORESIGHT during your adventure, you may employ it here to find out whether or not the bread is safe to eat. To do this, place the FORESIGHT

POWER CARD exactly over the 'eye' shape below. If you haven't been given the **POWER OF FORESIGHT**, you'll have to hope for the best in making your decision about the bread.

If you decide to eat it   **go to 11**
If you decide to avoid it   **go to 261**

34

As you're lowering yourself to the bottom, the cage again gives a disconcerting jolt. It sounds as if another of the rope's strands have snapped. So you proceed as slowly and gently as possible, careful not to make any sudden movement in the cage. When you finally reach the bottom of the shaft, you quickly examine the rope. There's only one strand still intact and even this looks as if it would have given way at any moment! You now check the ropes on the other three cages. When you have found the cage that seems the safest, you begin your second ascent of the shaft. ***Go to 247.***

'Where am I? What happened?' you ask in confusion as your eyes focus on a sniggering goblin. His close-set features show that he takes great pleasure in your enfeebled state. 'You were chased by a fireball, that's what happened!' he cackles. 'You should have seen yourself! You passed out right in front of it. It's lucky for you that the fireball suddenly stopped and started to roll backwards.' **Go to 128.**

36
THIS CREATURE
IS SLAIN BY

WOUNDS

Wage combat by simultaneously throwing the two dice. If you slay the creature, go to 263. If the creature inflicts a wound on you first, deduct 1 from your STRENGTH RATING and then flee well away from this region by hurrying to 12.

37

As you step towards the bubble on the right, the double trapped in there becomes even more frantic. He starts to use his teeth on the tough, transparent skin, his eyes huge with fear. The air in there is obviously running out. You indicate to him to step to one side so you can thrust your sword into the bubble. The moment you puncture it, though, there is a massive explosion which sends you flying into the tunnel wall. You're badly injured and dazed, only just conscious enough to realise that this has all been a massive trap . . .

Deduct 1 from your STRENGTH RATING. Go next to 272.

38

'Who knows where we're going?' the old man answers you ironically, his crusted eyes still on the ground. 'The young ones go in search of work and wages to support their families. Old ones like me just hope for a little food now and then. Our village was once the richest in this kingdom, right next to the diamond mine. But since Draxun has filled it with his monsters it has become the poorest. Oh! Would that someone had the courage to go down the mine again and defy his terrible fiends!' When you tell the old man that that is precisely your mission, he is at first disbelieving. But then he glances up and notices your sword, shield – and muscular limbs. Although he still doesn't seem to give you much hope, he now at least takes you seriously. 'If that be so,' he says, looking furtively all about him, 'then I can probably be of some assistance to you.' *Go to 119.*

39

The next creature you encounter, some two hundred metres further along the tunnel, also won't step too close to the wall of fire. For all its ferocious taunting and howling, the fiend seems nervous of it. Or, again, is it just Murgle that it is nervous of? From your safe distance, you take stock of both this creature and the diamond it protects. With a huge horn in the centre of its head and a serrated

scimitar in its claw, the creature is quite awe-inspiring. But then so is the diamond! It sparkles not just white and blue but also yellow and red, the leap of the flames imprisoned in some of its mirror-like facets.

If you wish to fight creature	**go to 218**
If you wish to avoid it	**go to 70**

40

Your last sword-thrust was deadly accurate; passing right between two of the scorpion's brittle segments and finding its soft innards. The steel of your blade turns fatally there, wringing an agonised wail from the creature. The moment the sword is withdrawn, the creature drops, dead, to the ground. It collapses right on top of the diamond, though, and you have to roll the foul body away to reach the gem. The thought of having to touch that oozing corpse makes you feel nauseous, so you use your feet instead. At least you have the protection of your hide boots there. Finally, you're able to slide the diamond out and you triumphantly drop it into your haversack.

Add 1 to the score on your TREASURE COUNTER. Now hurry well away from this region by going to 5.

41

The spectre disappears, its white wisps evaporating into the darkness, as you tug at the loose rock in the middle. As soon as it is free, you drop it to the ground and eagerly insert your hand into the cavity. Unable to feel anything, you thrust your arm even deeper . . . up to your elbow, then the shoulder. But still your fingers don't touch anything and you finally accept that you chose the wrong rock. You quickly pull your arm out again, hoping to get a grip on one of the others before it seals into the wall as the spectre had warned. But you're too late. There's just a solid wall of rock in front of you. **Go to 301.**

42

The sorcerer's manic stare switches from you to a small niche in the rock to your left. 'You will see there three drinking horns,' he snarls. 'One contains white wine, one red and one green. Two of these wines have been laced with a strength-sapping potion. The other is harmless. You must drink from one of these horns or you will immediately be struck dead by a bolt of lightning!' So you reluctantly step towards the niche, noticing that each horn is engraved with the same strange cipher: ✳.

If you have picked up the BOOK OF CIPHERS during your adventure, you may consult it here to find out what the cipher means. If not, you'll have to hope for the best in making your choice between the three wines.

If you choose white wine	**go to 151**
If you choose red wine	**go to 206**
If you choose green wine	**go to 110**

43

As the creature drops heavily to the ground, its face contorted, howling in agony, you immediately start to look around for the diamond. You move from one wall of the cave to another, expecting something to sparkle at any moment, but there's only the coarse blackness of the rock. Surely you haven't risked your life with that awesome creature for nothing? The precious jewel must be somewhere – but where? Just as you're about to leave the cave, full of despair, you spot the diamond. It forms the 'ball' of the creature's mace! As you wrench the precious but lethally-hard stone from its chain, you realise how lucky you were. If that mace had once struck you during combat, the blow would surely have done you great injury or even been fatal.

Add 1 to the score on your TREASURE COUNTER. Now hurry well away from this cavern by going to 289.

44
THIS CREATURE
IS SLAIN BY

WOUNDS

Wage combat by simultaneously throwing the two dice. If you slay the creature, go to 321. If the creature inflicts a wound on you first, deduct 1 from your STRENGTH RATING and then flee well away from this region by hurrying to 12.

45
You haven't followed this right branch of the tunnel far when you spot two tiny points of green light in the darkness ahead. They seem to be a pair of eyes and you immediately draw out your sword. Eyes

that shine as piercingly as that surely can't belong to any benevolent being! 'Return your sword to its sheath!' a voice commands as the eyes gradually approach out of the darkness and an aged, long-bearded face appears round them. 'I intend you no harm and, even if I did, your sword would be futile against me. I am a sorcerer. If I so wished, with a glance I could turn your sword towards your heart. But I am here to help you.' Do you trust the sorcerer – or do you ignore him and hurry onwards?

| If trust him | **go to 318** |
| If hurry onwards | **go to 99** |

46

You're about halfway up the rope on the right – several metres from the ground – when something disconcerting happens. The rope starts to be pulled up. And it's being pulled up far too fast for it to be anyone trying to help you! Your elbows and knees are instantly ripped open on the rough surface of the rock. Realising that there's something hostile waiting up there for you, you quickly try to descend the rope. But those unseen hands pull you up even faster than you can climb down. Your elbows now severely gashed, you find it impossible to keep a grip on the rope. You drop helplessly to the hard ground below . . .

Deduct 1 from your STRENGTH RATING. Go next to 130.

It's not much longer before you reach another portcullis along this tunnel . . . and another creature snarling at you from behind it. The creature's foul appearance makes you take a couple of steps back in horror. The abomination seems to be *inside out*: its body being made up of soft, coiled entrails and its head of an enlarged brain. It doesn't appear to possess a single bone! You start to

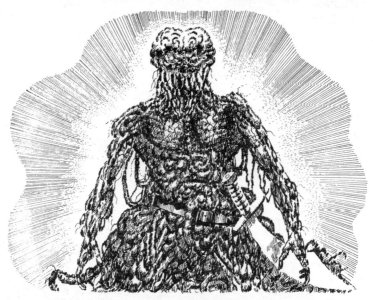

wonder whether there might be advantage for you in this, however. Your sword would surely go straight through the creature. Wounding it would be so easy. But then you notice the vicious looking scimitar hanging from the creature's 'hip'. One lunge from that would surely go straight through *you* as well!

If you wish to fight creature	**go to 241**
If you wish to avoid it	**go to 29**

The entire mine seeming to echo with its agonised howl, the creature staggers back from your last sword-thrust. The hideous fiend crumples to its knees and then keels over on to its left side. You immediately snatch up its heavy, curved sword, using the thick point to try and winkle out the diamond from the rock. You grin in delight as the priceless stone finally comes loose from the tunnel wall.

Add 1 to the score on your TREASURE COUNTER. Now hurry well away from this region by going to 27.

49

The old hag spits and curses at you, her leathery face contorted in hate. But you're not at all intimidated by this. Indeed, you're quite happy to be subject to it for it shows that you spoke her name correctly. As bitter as she is, the hag remains true to her word. With a snake-like tongue she starts to lick the slime off you. Although this repulsive lapping makes you squirm and quiver, you immediately feel the strength start to flow back into your body.

Add 1 to your STRENGTH RATING. Go next to 4.

50

If any of the shovels *do* have a curse on them, then it must be one of the other two. For the shovel you have chosen allows you gradually to work your way through the rocks. The obstruction now removed, you take a quick rest before continuing your exploration of the tunnel. As you are resting, though, you become aware of something moving near your feet. Then it starts to coil round your ankles. You nervously glance down, assuming it to be a snake. But it's something much more terrifying than that. It's the shovel! *Go to 293.*

51
THIS CREATURE
IS SLAIN BY

WOUNDS

Wage combat by simultaneously throwing the two dice. If you slay the creature, go to 186. If the creature inflicts a wound on you first, deduct 1 from your STRENGTH RATING and then flee well away from this region by hurrying to 281.

52

The tunnel goes on and on, still so large that it's more like a cavern. But then it splits in two – quite literally. There is now a deep ravine running straight through the middle of the tunnel. You will have to keep either to the right or the left – for although the ravine is not very wide, it's just wide enough to prevent you crossing from one side to the other as you follow it. Which side of the ravine will you choose?

If left side	**go to 176**
If right side	**go to 225**

The demon-like creature falls right in front of you, snorting black smoke from its nostrils. It continues to emit this smoke as it writhes on the ground but with less and less force, the puffs becoming fewer and fewer. They soon cease altogether and you know that the creature is dead. You chip the diamond from the tunnel wall, and transfer the magnificent stone to your haversack. It feels good to know that you took this huge risk, that you put Queen Tarsha and her starving people first.

*Add 1 to the score on your **TREASURE COUNTER**. Now hurry well away from this region by going to 12.*

As you return to the edge of the three pools, you wonder which one to try now. Suddenly, though, the mist hovering above the middle one lifts. Moreover, the water completely loses its murkiness, becoming crystal-clear. *This* surely has to be the pool you should choose. You therefore wade into it, immediately feeling a strange sensation in your weakened body. Is it becoming even weaker or is the weakness departing? To your delight, it proves to be the latter. You wade out of the pool again, feeling completely revitalised.

*Add 1 to your **STRENGTH RATING**. Go next to 328.*

Your eyes slowly focus on a maiden standing in front of you in a long white gown. She seems to be made of ice: her hair and lashes frosted and her flesh a gleaming ice blue. You wonder if the hazy figure really *is* there – or if it's just your dazed mind playing tricks. She then speaks, however. 'I am the spirit Vulelia,' she says in a voice as quiet as falling snow. 'Take either my left or right hand to pull yourself to your feet. One hand will immediately restore the strength you have lost. But I cannot tell you which . . . and you may only take the one.'

If you have been taught the TRANCE SPELL during your adventure, you may cast it here to hypnotise the spirit into disclosing the correct hand to take. To do this, place the TRANCE SPELL CARD exactly over the spirit's 'mind square' below. If you haven't been taught the TRANCE SPELL, you'll have to hope for the best in making your choice.

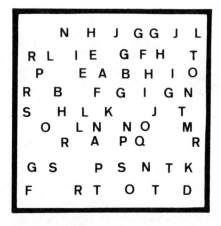

If you choose left hand   **go to 327**
If you choose right hand   **go to 279**

56

Keeping to the very centre of the tunnel, you continue your journey into the shadows. They twist and turn ahead of you; sometimes black, sometimes a dingy flickering yellow. Every so often you think there's a monster lurking in these shadows but it's just your anxiety playing tricks on your mind. This section of the mine, at least, proves to be without danger. *Go to 221.*

The goblin snarls at you for refusing his assistance, giving the flimsy birdcage a furious and cruel shake. 'Then be it on your own head!' he shrieks. 'Without my canary, the first you'll know of the explosive gases is when they blow you to smithereens!' You still refuse to trust either him or the canary, however, and you continue your journey down this part of the tunnel. Not once do the lamps suddenly start to burn more fiercely than normal. Not once do you have the slightest whiff of gas. The goblin was clearly trying to alarm you unnecessarily! *Go to 236.*

58
THIS CREATURE
IS SLAIN BY

WOUNDS

Wage combat by simultaneously throwing the two dice. If you slay the creature, go to 117. If the creature inflicts a wound on you first, deduct 1 from your STRENGTH RATING and then flee well away from this region by hurrying to 29.

59

The slain creature hits the ground with such force that you half expect the rock to crack beneath it. Certainly, the ground seems to shudder a little. You immediately wrench the spear from the creature's hand and snap off its sharp head. This is the perfect tool to chip the diamond free from the tunnel wall. When the sparkling stone finally comes loose, you find that it is even bigger than it appeared. It's the size of your fist; surely worth almost a kingdom in itself!

Add 1 to the score on your TREASURE COUNTER. Now hurry well away from this region by going to 281.

60

The creature's skin appears to be of almost impenetrable leather and even this is protected at the shoulders and chest by thick chain-mail. There's also iron protection on its head, where sits a spiked

helmet. But that's all just to *defend* the creature. The manic, red-eyed being also has something equally daunting with which to attack; a glinting broadsword. It grins hideously as, to demonstrate the blade's sharpness, it swings the weapon at a huge cobweb. The blade slices clean through the centre of the web – without causing a single thread to pull away from its support!

If you wish to fight creature	**go to 25**
If you wish to avoid it	**go to 134**

61

You hold your breath as the lamp slave gradually opens his palm. It's completely unmarked. You briefly see him shake his head woefully before he disappears, the lamps ahead of you suddenly extinguishing. You slowly and anxiously move forwards in the darkness, trying to estimate the position of the extinguished lamps. You calculate that you should have reached at least twenty of the thirty by now – perhaps even more. Suddenly, though, you find yourself falling down a pothole . . . *Go to 278.*

62
THIS CREATURE
IS SLAIN BY

WOUNDS

Wage combat by simultaneously throwing the two dice. If you slay the creature, go to 82. If the creature inflicts a wound on you first, deduct 1 from your STRENGTH RATING and then flee well away from this region by hurrying to 29.

63

You're beginning to wonder whether you were right to hurry past that last creature – even though it was quite the most repulsive thing you've seen so far. For there appear to be no more monsters in this particular section of the mine. Which means, of course, no more diamonds either. But then you hear *yet another* creature bellowing some distance ahead. Your heart almost leaps at the sound! When the monster finally comes into view, however, it's a very different story. Your heart instantly freezes . . . *Go to 257.*

64

As you touch its cold slimy surface, tiny tremors start to pass from the skull to your fingers. They travel all the way up your arm to the rest of your body. You hope that this is doing you good but you soon realise that, far from restoring your strength, the tremors are actually sapping it. You desperately try to withdraw your hand but you find that you haven't the strength. As you grow weaker and weaker, your only hope is that the hideous skull doesn't intend to finish you off altogether . . .

Deduct 1 from your STRENGTH RATING. Go next to 197.

65

The white-gowned clone points to two tiny fountains that have suddenly sprung from the ground, one to your left and one to your right. 'If you drink of the correct one,' she tells you, 'then it will be as if the fungi had never weakened you. But the other fountain is merely water and will do no more than refresh you a little. Choose now, for the fountains will soon vanish again.'

If you have been taught the TRANCE SPELL during your adventure, you may cast it here to hypnotise the clone into telling you which is the correct fountain. To do this, place the TRANCE SPELL CARD exactly over the clone's 'mind square' below. If you haven't been taught the TRANCE SPELL, you'll have to hope for the best in making your decision.

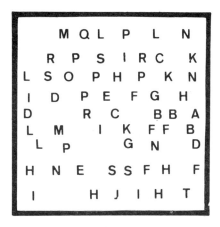

If you choose fountain to your left   **go to 180**
If you choose fountain to your right   **go to 143**

66

You haven't ventured far into this tunnel when you hear a deafening roar. You peer into the dim light snaking ahead, from one lamp to the next, trying to identify the source of the noise. But it must be coming from much further ahead than you can see, from round the distant bend. And as soon as you turn this bend, you come face to face with the cause. Across the entrance to a large recess at the side of the tunnel there is a sturdy portcullis. This recess is home to a magnificent diamond – and a terrifying ape-like creature . . . *Go to 19.*

You pull your hand quickly away from the double, almost certain that he cannot be trusted. For one thing, how did he manage to survive the bubble completely unscathed? One moment he was desperately trying to claw his way out and the next he is right as rain standing above you! Were his frantic pleas from inside the bubble just to lure *you* in there too? But then you begin to wonder whether he is genuinely trying to help after all. He doesn't seem at all angered by your rejection of his hand – just saddened. It's too late to change your mind, though. For the double suddenly vanishes into thin air. ***Go to 197.***

68
THIS CREATURE
IS SLAIN BY

WOUNDS

Wage combat by simultaneously throwing the two dice. If you slay the creature, go to 161. If the creature inflicts a wound on you first, deduct 1 from your STRENGTH RATING and then flee well away from this region by hurrying to 29.

Turning round, you see that there are three men standing there with pickaxes over their shoulders. 'My name is Gurn,' the man in the centre says, 'and this is Lekk and Nabel. We are all miners and we have hidden down here so that we can carry out small acts of sabotage wherever we can. We lay crude traps for the monsters. We cause squabbles between them. But enough of that for the moment. There's something much more important that you should know . . .' ***Go to 310.***

There can be no doubt that the next creature you encounter is nervous of the wall of fire. Its head and body are of ice! There's a hood over this head (for insulation, you assume) but you can still see the ghastly ice-eyes and grinning ice-teeth beneath. Even the

creature's weapon is of ice; a stout, sharpened icicle. Although you can't yet spot the diamond it protects, you're sure there must be one somewhere nearby. The creature's grotesque smirking grin seems to tell you that. So you try and taunt the fiend towards you, a little closer to the wall of fire. But it's not as gullible as you'd hoped, remaining exactly where it is. Clearly the only way you're going to destroy it is not by cunning – but by taking it on in battle.

If you wish to fight creature	**go to 291**
If you wish to avoid it	**go to 323**

71

You step unscathed through the puff of green smoke. The dense vapours don't suddenly turn poisonous . . . nor do they try and ensnare you. That you chose the correct puff of smoke seems to be confirmed by a tiny snarling voice emitted from its centre. It's the enraged gnome. But the voice gradually fades away and, afterwards, so too does the smoke. *Go to 197.*

72

Passing through the door on the right, you find yourself staring at a broad wooden pole with ancient carvings all the way up it. It must have been a whole tree-trunk because its circumference is a good five metres. But what surprises you even more is its height. That's at least fifteen metres. You can't see how this is possible given that this part of the tunnel is at the most only about half that height! You decide not to dwell on this, though, giving your attention instead to those intricate carvings. They all seem to be of monsters with snarling teeth and bulbous eyes. Your gaze climbs from one to the next, finally reaching the most grotesque of all at the top. But then you suddenly catch your breath . . . *Go to 167.*

73

'That was the last fork in the tunnel,' Gurn informs you. 'Your path now is direct. I must return to my friends to help them try and clear those rock-falls. Good luck!' As he hurriedly disappears back towards the cavern, however, you wonder whether this is all a trap. Your anxieties increase when you notice an ominous-looking cryptic on the tunnel wall: **XXYXXYY**. It's written in blood! Is this a warning about grave dangers ahead?

If you have picked up the CRYPTICS SCROLL during your adventure, you may consult it here to find out what the cryptic means. If not, you'll have to hope for the best in deciding whether you should continue or not.

If you decide to continue	**go to 240**
If you decide to make your way back	**go to 160**

74

Dragging your aching body towards the centre of the tunnel, you anxiously wait for the next flash of lightning to strike. If your choice is wrong, of course, then the lightning might weaken you even further. That's if it doesn't kill you! In fact it has absolutely no effect; neither strengthening nor weakening you. It makes you wonder how real these forms of lightning are. Could they be just a figment of your dazed mind? Your mind is becoming a little clearer now, though, and your body not quite so stiff. You struggle to your feet and move over towards the left of the tunnel in preparation for the next flash of lightning. Unfortunately, though, that was the very last of them. *Go to 197.*

75

As you peer into this huge man-made hole, into the hollow darkness within, you can't see anything of the fiends that are supposed to inhabit it. Nor can you hear anything. At the very least, you expect the occasional wail to echo towards you, but there's nothing. Just a strange, unnerving silence. Anxious, you enter that hollow darkness, glad to find that it is soon relieved by a trail of lamps. The lamps appear only occasionally, and their amber glow is by no means strong, but at least you can just about make out where you are going. For a while you walk in a horizontal line, the wide tunnel seeming no more than a short-cut through the crag. But then, after boring some three hundred metres or so into the mountain, the tunnel suddenly terminates at a large cavern. *Go to 284.*

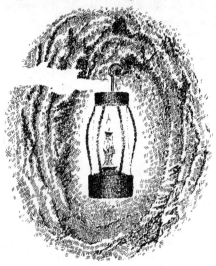

76

Pulling on its rope, you heave this cage further and further up the shaft. You estimate that you have raised yourself at least fifteen metres by now, perhaps even more. Suddenly, however, the cage halts. It would appear that the rope from which it is suspended is starting to fray! Fortunately, this seems to be happening quite slowly for the moment and you wonder whether the rope will hold out until you reach the top of the shaft. But you don't know how much further the top *is*. It could be a good thirty metres for all you know. Perhaps even fifty. If that's the case, it would be far more prudent to lower yourself to the bottom again and use one of the other cages.

If you have acquired the POWER OF FORESIGHT during your adventure, you may employ it here to find out whether the cage would make it to the top or not. To do this, place the

FORESIGHT POWER CARD exactly over the 'eye' shape below. If you haven't acquired FORESIGHT POWER, you'll have to hope for the best in making your decision.

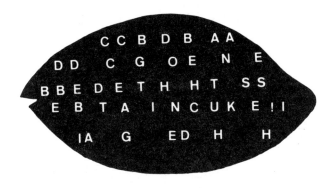

If you decide to risk continuing   **go to 199**
If you decide to return to shaft bottom   **go to 34**

77

You have a fright as the slain creature crashes to the ground. The cave shudders so violently that for a moment it looks as if the portcullis will come sliding down again with you trapped inside. But, despite a few vibrations, the portcullis stays raised. The fright still causes you to work quickly at removing the diamond, however. You hack feverishly at the rock with your sword, sometimes using the blade, sometimes using the hilt. As soon as the precious stone comes free, you hurry to the other side of the portcullis again; back into the safety of the tunnel.

Add 1 to the score on your TREASURE COUNTER. Now hurry well away from this region by going to 29.

78

Although you hurry after Nabel, down this left branch of the tunnel, you don't follow quite as close as you did before. You keep a few more paces between you. After witnessing that strange division

Nabel underwent, you no longer completely trust him. You start to wonder if he's leading you into a trap. So you carefully tread exactly where he does in case there are any hidden pitfalls along the tunnel. In spite of this caution, you suddenly find yourself falling into a large pothole . . . *Go to 275.*

79

This one is like a huge, upright scorpion. Its body is of brittle segments and both hands and feet take the form of pincers. But there's also something partly human in the creature, for it is able to hold a slender sword in those pincers and its brandishing of that sword is skilful. Nevertheless, the creature still doesn't look totally

agile on its pincer feet and you are sure it would be fairly easy to slip past it. If you did, though, you would be leaving behind a *second* treasure. For the creature stands astride a diamond even bigger than the previous one.

If you wish to fight creature   **go to 207**
If you wish to avoid it   **go to 109**

80

You choose the goblet on the left because the swirling vapour rises thickest from that one. This would surely suggest that the potion underneath is the most powerful. When you try to sip it through the vapour, however, you find that there isn't actually any potion underneath. The potion is the vapour itself. Even so, you eventually realise that it was the *wrong* potion. You've now waited a good ten minutes since swallowing all the vapour but still your body has all those terrible aches and bruises. At least you can just manage to walk, though, and so you painfully continue in the direction which Gurn showed you. *Go to 123.*

81
THIS CREATURE
IS SLAIN BY

WOUNDS

Wage combat by simultaneously throwing the two dice. If you slay the creature, go to 126. If the creature inflicts a wound on you first, deduct 1 from your STRENGTH RATING and then escape from the pyramid by going to 282.

Tugging your sword out of the creature's leathery flesh, you wait for it to slump to the ground. This happens slowly, but at last it drops to its knees and keels over. Its eyes take on a glassy stare – but you wonder whether this is no more than a return to the temporarily frozen state it was in before. When you testingly move the tip of your sword to the diamond, however, the creature fails even to blink. This time it really is dead. So you use your sword more purposefully, chipping away the rock round the magnificent gemstone, which eventually drops into your hand.

Add 1 to the score on your TREASURE COUNTER. Now hurry well away from this region by going to 29.

83

Your eyes are so riveted to the massive diamond that it takes you a while to notice the several creatures straining in the darkness at the base of the pyramid. There seems to be one chained to each of the pyramid's three sides; their duty obviously each to protect that particular approach to the diamond. You cautiously step a pace or two forwards, trying to obtain a clearer view of the creature that is nearest you . . . ***Go to 211.***

84

You haven't followed this right branch of the tunnel far when you notice a large inscription chiselled into its rocky wall. You try to read it but there's only the dimmest flicker of light on it. Most of it is lost in shadow. So you unhook the nearest of the lamps, bringing it right up to the inscription. You can now see it quite clearly: **XYXYYXX**. It appears to be some sort of cryptic and you're convinced that it must be giving a warning. Perhaps about which side of the tunnel you should keep to from now on.

If you have picked up the CRYPTICS SCROLL during your adventure, you may consult it here to find out the inscription's warning. If not, you'll have to make a guess at it.

<blockquote>

If you think it means
    KEEP TO LEFT   **go to 185**
If you think it means
    KEEP TO CENTRE   **go to 56**
If you think it means
    KEEP TO RIGHT   **go to 297**

</blockquote>

85

'You're wrong!' the goblin on the right screeches gleefully. 'I am the *truthful* one!' You anxiously put a hand to your sword, wondering what their penalty will be. Will they suddenly kick your cage so it crashes into the opposite wall of the shaft? Will they suddenly produce a dagger and sever the rope that holds it? But then you realise that perhaps your answer wasn't wrong after all. Although the goblin on the right said that it was wrong, that's just what you would expect him to say if he is the one that always tells lies! It seems that your reasoning is correct, for the goblins don't take any action against you at all, allowing you to continue your progress up the shaft. *Go to 247.*

'A good question!' the bearded man says, laughing wretchedly, as you ask him where he is going. His dejected eyes only half lift to look at you and his laugh is short and bitter. 'Where *does* a diamond miner go when he can't work his mine any more? There are no other mines in this land – and it is probably far too late for me to learn any other trade. I tell you, I'm half inclined to stay and curse right in the face of Draxun's terrible monsters. But I don't have the courage, of course. So what can I do but abandon the mine?' As the bearded man plods resignedly past you, the rest of the small exodus tramping behind him, you become even more determined to succeed at your quest. You hate to think of these innocent people victimised so cruelly by Draxun. ***Go to 209.***

First the creature's studded club thuds to the ground . . . and then the creature itself. It lies there paralysed, its grotesque eyes staring straight at you. You wait for them to close before attempting to remove the diamond from its palm. As soon as they do, you act quickly before the dead fingers stiffen round the jewel. It's the most beautiful specimen you've ever seen, the glinting facets almost without need of cutting. Nature seems to have done the work already.

Add 1 to the score on your TREASURE COUNTER. Now hurry well away from this region by going to 5.

You soon come across another creature in this tunnel – and this one is asleep, too. Again it sleeps just below the large diamond set loosely in the tunnel wall. You're sure that you could extract the precious stone using only your fingers . . . but you are more cautious this time. Your hand slowly approaches the diamond, fraction by fraction, ready to whip back again the moment there's any sound. At the same time you carefully watch the creature's leathery eyelids. There appear to be two monstrous eyeballs underneath, bulging like a frog's. Your heart jumps as the wail starts up briefly and the creature slowly raises one eyelid.

Fortunately, though, you're quick enough to stop it again before fully waking the creature. But wake it you obviously must if you want your hand to get any nearer to the diamond . . .

If you wish to fight creature   **go to 250**
If you wish to avoid it   **go to 229**

89

Although the climb is very difficult and several times you nearly lose your footing, you at last reach the top of the pole. You steady yourself there, inserting one foot into the carved monster's mouth and resting the other on one of its huge warts. Then with anguish you suddenly realise that you have nothing with which to prise out the diamond. You have of course left your sword at the bottom of the pole, so that it wouldn't impede your climb. You're just about to make the long climb down again, however, when the diamond miraculously starts to turn. It seems to be unscrewing itself from the wood! Moments later it drops safely into your cupped hands.

Add 1 to the score on your TREASURE COUNTER. Go next to 298.

90
THIS CREATURE
IS SLAIN BY

WOUNDS

Wage combat by simultaneously throwing the two dice. If you slay the creature, go to 210. If the creature inflicts a wound on you first, deduct 1 from your STRENGTH RATING and then flee well away from this cavern by hurrying to 289.

91
Leading away from the bottom of the shaft is a horizontal tunnel and you assume that this is the start of the diamond mine. The shaft was just to get the workers down to this mine. And the large cavern

above the shaft was probably a collection area, where the workers handed over their finds to be graded. You had noticed several rusty pairs of scales up there, and an assortment of sieves. Yes, it's only now that you can expect to come across the diamonds . . . and you eagerly follow this new tunnel, relieved to see that the trail of lamps starts to guide you again. *Go to 132.*

92

To your relief, the tunnel soon becomes more secure again. As you proceed, the ominous creaking fades away and the showers of dust become finer and finer. Five hundred metres from the rock-fall the flames of the lamps burning on the walls are perfectly steady once more. But it's then that you notice a hazy apparition a short distance in front of you, an apparition so eerie it freezes your blood . . . *Go to 330.*

93

As you rather anxiously glance round at the three gnomes, you realise that they are all exactly the same. They even have the same strange cipher embroidered on their hoods: ✵. You're just wondering about this cipher when each gnome suddenly turns into a thick puff of smoke; one white, one blue and one green. Encircled by these, you can only break free of them by stepping through one of the puffs of smoke. But which do you choose? Perhaps that cipher on the gnomes' hoods provided a clue.

If you have picked up the BOOK OF CIPHERS during your

adventure, you may consult it here to find out what the cipher means. If not, you'll have to hope for the best in deciding which puff of smoke to step through.

If you choose white smoke   **go to 195**
If you choose blue smoke   **go to 255**
If you choose green smoke   **go to 71**

94

As you swallow the potion, the goblin's face falls. Again, you're not sure of the reason for this. You hope that it's because you chose the strength-*restoring* potion but maybe it's just because you didn't choose the strength-*reducing* one. You eventually realise that unfortunately this is the case for, although you are now able to stand up, you're still feeling just as groggy. *Go to 254.*

95

Not really sure how, you finally manage to claw your way to the top of the hole. You force your gashed and aching arms to make one last almighty effort and you heave yourself out. You allow yourself a few minutes to recover from your exertions before continuing along the pitch-black tunnel. You proceed even more carefully this time, just in case there are further potholes. Fortunately, there aren't – and you at last reach the illuminated part of the tunnel again. *Go to 18.*

You start to follow the white-gowned figure, confident that *she* is the original Guardian Spirit of the mine and the one who will guide you safely through the next part of the mine. You did see her first, after all. She keeps beckoning you, finger over her shoulder, leading you towards the extreme right of the large tunnel. As you squeeze along this rough wall, however, you suddenly feel something sucking at your shoulder . . . ***Go to 216.***

The creature's eyes watch you closely as you edge away from it, as close to the fiery ravine as you dare. You wonder if the ghastly

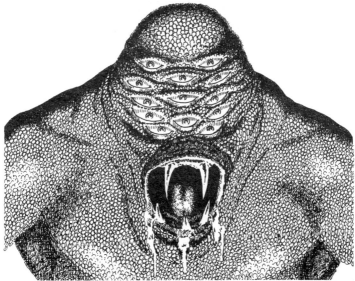

creature will force you into combat. But it remains pressed against the side of the tunnel, seeming nervous of the flames. Or maybe it's Murgle's wrath that it is nervous about. For you now spot the magnificent diamond that the creature has to protect, sparkling in the coarse rock just behind it.

If you wish to fight creature   **go to 226**
If you wish to avoid it   **go to 319**

Just as your first sword-strike completely severed the neck of the *right* head of the creature, your second strike completely severs its *left* one. The twice-decapitated fiend immediately collapses to the ground. Although it continues to twitch for a while, you know that this is merely a post-death twitch and the creature can do you no further harm. You immediately step towards the brilliant sparkle in the rock-face. After chipping the diamond free with your sword, you transfer it to your haversack.

Add 1 to the score on your TREASURE COUNTER. Now hurry well away from this region by going to 27.

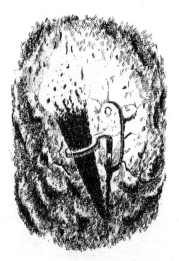

99

This branch of the tunnel soon joins up with the other one again and you are once more following quite a wide passageway. But just as wide is a dark crater you suddenly encounter in the tunnel floor! It stretches from one side of the tunnel to the other and you're not sure how you're going to cross it. You have three options. First, you can descend into the crater, hoping that it is not as deep as it looks. Second, you can try and make your way round the edge by hanging on to the rocks that jut out from the tunnel wall. Or third, you can attempt to leap right across it! All are perilous, but you're going to have to decide on *one* of these courses of action. Which will it be?

If you have acquired the POWER OF FORESIGHT during your adventure, you may employ it here to find out which course of action to take. To do this, place the FORESIGHT POWER CARD exactly over the 'eye' shape below. If you haven't acquired FORESIGHT POWER, you'll have to hope for the best in deciding which branch to take.

If descend into crater   **go to 3**
If scramble round its edge   **go to 179**
If try to leap across   **go to 258**

100
THIS CREATURE
IS SLAIN BY

WOUNDS

Wage combat by simultaneously throwing the two dice. If you slay the creature, go to 7. If the creature inflicts a wound on you first, deduct 1 from your STRENGTH RATING and then flee well away from this cavern by hurrying to 289.

101

Eyes full of hatred, the creature slumps to the ground at your feet. That hatred still stares at you even after the fiend has gasped its last breath. Either it has no eyelids, or the eyelids refuse to give you comfort. So you turn your anguished gaze away from the monster, switching it to the diamond. With a couple of gentle blows from your sword, you loosen the jewel from the tunnel wall and straightaway place it in your haversack so you can move on from this unsettling scene.

Add 1 to the score on your TREASURE COUNTER. Now hurry well away from this region by going to 12.

102

The lamp slave slowly opens his right palm. There's an ugly black cross gouged into its centre. 'You have chosen wisely, my friend,' he says. 'Your path will continue to have illumination. And I wish you luck. Although I am an agent of the sorcerer Murgle, I am an enforced agent. His spell ensures that I can never be free of this lamp. But I hope that *you* will soon be free of this mine.' *Go to 18.*

103

You wonder which of the two branches Nabel will choose, but the answer is *both*! Something quite extraordinary now happens to him. He separates into two! One Nabel starts to walk down the left branch of the tunnel and the other starts to walk down the right. Your mind is quite stupefied by this but you have to put this amazement aside for the time being. The two Nabels are fast disappearing down their respective tunnels. If you don't want to be left there, you're going to have to follow one of them.

If you have acquired the POWER OF FORESIGHT during your adventure, you may employ it here to find out which is the correct Nabel to follow. To do this, place the FORESIGHT POWER CARD exactly over the 'eye' shape below. If you haven't acquired FORESIGHT POWER, you'll have to hope for the best in deciding which branch to take.

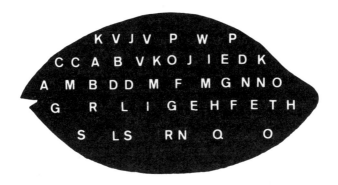

If you choose branch on left   **go to 78**
If you choose branch on right   **go to 242**

104

You tentatively set to work with the shovel you have chosen, wondering if it will suddenly turn against you. But it remains obediently in your hands as you slowly dig a way through the massive pile of rocks. Then, suddenly, your digging starts to grow faster and faster. It's not you that's doing it but the shovel, and you desperately try to release it as its frantic action rapidly exhausts your muscles. But it seems to be welded to your hands, forcing your arms to go along with its frenzy. Within minutes you have dug a channel right through the rock-fall. But you are so weak from your frenzied exertions that you'll be lucky if you can make use of this path . . .

Deduct 1 from your STRENGTH RATING. Go next to 198.

105
THIS CREATURE
IS SLAIN BY

WOUNDS

Wage combat by simultaneously throwing the two dice. If you slay the creature, go to 259. If the creature inflicts a wound on you first, deduct 1 from your STRENGTH RATING and then flee well away from this region by hurrying to 27.

106

As you step into the pool in the centre, both its murkiness and the slight mist hovering over it clear. You can now see right to its bottom, and it is not nearly as deep as you had feared. Nor is it scalding hot or icy cold. The water comes up to your knees – and it's soothingly warm. As you safely reach the other side of the pool, you wonder what dangers lurk in the other two! *Go to 328.*

107

Fortunately, your arm does hold out long enough for you to reach the top of the crater. And, also fortunately, the poison *wasn't* deadly. Although your arm still feels drained of strength, at least that numbness hasn't spread to the rest of your body. You can still proceed with your quest! ***Go to 239.***

108

You put the earmuffs over your head, pressing the fur cups against your ears. Only seconds later you hear a hideous piercing scream coming through them. Clamping your hands over the muffs as well, however, you can just about block out most of this. When the awful wail has finally subsided, you try to imagine how much worse it would have been if you *hadn't* been wearing the muffs. It would almost certainly have driven you insane! ***Go to 328.***

109

As you had hoped, you manage to slip past the scorpion creature quite easily. You make as if you're going to try and pass to its right but at the last moment you switch to its left. It's unable to turn quickly enough and you flee deeper into the tunnel. Again the creature doesn't give chase . . . but, again, you're soon encountering another. ***Go to 188.***

110

When you have drained the wine from the goblet, you tensely wait to see if it has any effect. The signs seem to be good because Murgle is completely quiet. Surely, if you had chosen one of the drugged wines, his manic cackle would have immediately started up again? But then it does. He has deliberately lulled you into a false hope. As his spiteful laughter becomes louder and louder, your body grows weaker and weaker . . .

Deduct 1 from your STRENGTH RATING. Go next to 206.

111

Seeing how you keep your hand back from it, the skull gives a hideous menacing grin. It's clearly not pleased that you refused to trust it. The grin becomes more and more evil-looking and the eye sockets grow blacker and blacker, deeper and deeper. The skull then starts to hover towards you. Certain now that contact with it would be fatal, you desperately slide away from it, across the ground. But then the skull suddenly disappears. Its menace has gone. *Go to 197.*

112

You haven't limped far from the pool when you spot a series of letters gouged into the tunnel wall: **XXYYXXX**. They seem to be some sort of cryptic and you wonder whether it's telling you to return to one of the other two pools. Perhaps this will restore the strength you have lost. Or is the cryptic telling you the very opposite? Is it warning you to leave the area of the pools as quickly as possible?

If you have picked up the CRYPTICS SCROLL during your

adventure, you may consult it here to find out what the letters mean. If you haven't, you'll have to hope for the best in deciding what to do.

If you decide to return to pools	**go to 54**
If you decide to hurry onwards	**go to 328** .

113

The moment you have gripped the red sword, it starts to vibrate. This vibration becomes fiercer and fiercer, your whole arm shaking with it. Soon your entire body is trembling and you desperately try to release your hand from the sword. But it seems to be welded there and you rapidly weaken as the vibrations grow ever stronger and faster. Unless they stop soon, you're sure the demonic sword will be the end of you.

Deduct 1 from your STRENGTH RATING. Go next to 271.

114

You remain staring up at the pole for a while. You begin to wonder whether your decision not to climb it was the right one. The carved monsters look perfectly innocent still; without the slightest indication that they're suddenly going to come to life. You look guiltily at the diamond. Don't you owe it to Queen Tarsha and her starving kingdom to take the risk? So you again prepare to climb the pole. Just as you reach up for that first handhold, however, the pole disappears. You're too late! ***Go to 266.***

115

You drag your aching body towards the left side of the tunnel. You anxiously wait there for the next series of lightning flashes. Are you mad to do this? Did you *really* hear such an instruction? And, even if you did, why should you trust it? This could well be *another* trap, just like the bubble. The lightning may weaken you even further. It could, of course, even kill you. When it happens, however, it neither harms nor helps you. Just able to raise yourself to your feet now, you walk towards the centre of the tunnel to try your luck there. But unfortunately there is no more lightning. ***Go to 197.***

116

You hurried past that last diamond in the hope that the next one you came across would be protected by a slightly less terrifying guardian. Unfortunately, the next creature roars its taunts and wields its weapon with equal ferocity. It is horrendous in its appearance, with black horns sprouting from either side of its head.

In its clawed hand is a broken broadsword, the jagged edge purple with congealed blood. You again keep as close to the wall of fire as possible while you weigh up your chances of slaying the beast.

You're sure it would only be a very slim chance. But then how many more diamonds can you expect to find in this tunnel? Perhaps you owe it to Queen Tarsha and her starving people to take that slim chance . . .

If you wish to fight creature **go to 300**
If you wish to avoid it **go to 12**

117

The creature dies as silently as it lived. Not so much as a whimper escapes from it as you withdraw your sword from its innards. But the look it gives you as it crumples to the ground is as chilling as any blood-curdling howl. The slanted eyes are cruel and full of hatred. This chilling stare stays with you even after you have turned away from the fiend to hack out the diamond. You work as quickly as you can. You want to get well away from this unsettling place.

Add 1 to the score on your TREASURE COUNTER. Now hurry well away from this region by going to 29.

118

You keep anxiously glancing down at the floor of the cage as it continues its climb up the shaft. But the side you're standing on still feels perfectly secure. So you eventually assume you have chosen the safe side and take your eyes off the floor. But suddenly a huge hole opens at your feet and you fall straight through it. You just manage to grab hold of the bottom of the cage in time – but the crisis is far from over. Unless you can swing your legs back into the cage, you're going to be left dangling there. And with the weight of your whole body to support, your arms are already aching badly.

Deduct 1 from your STRENGTH RATING. Go next to 247.

119

The old man beckons you closer, explaining what he means. 'Although I might seem just an old man in rags,' he whispers into your ear, 'I am also a wizard. Never a very potent wizard, I admit, and even less so after all these years of near starvation. But I still have some powers left in me – and ones I know how to confer too!' He traces his fingertip across your forehead, outlining a diamond shape, then a square. 'You now have the power of foresight,' he tells you. 'It should greatly help you in your quest. Maybe – who knows? – even enough to succeed at it. I pray that it does.'

You may pick up the FORESIGHT POWER card. Go next to 209.

120

While you're still considering how best to pass the whirlwind, you notice that in the very centre of it there's a strange glowing symbol: ❖. It's a cipher of some sort and you wonder whether it is there to advise you.

If you have picked up the BOOK OF CIPHERS during your adventure, you may consult it here to find out what the symbol

means. If you haven't, you'll have to hope for the best in deciding how to pass the whirlwind.

If you decide on its right **go to 20**
If you decide on its left **go to 153**
If you decide through its middle **go to 267**

121

Stepping through the middle door, you find that the tunnel has suddenly become much larger. Its roof is now at least fifteen metres above you. As you are bewilderedly staring upwards at this, you spot three giant bubbles floating down from it. You are even more amazed when you notice what's inside the bubbles. For, as the bubbles finally come to rest on the ground, bouncing a little, you see that there is a human being trapped in each one. What really makes you gasp, though, is that in all three cases the human being is YOU! *Go to 253.*

122
THIS CREATURE
IS SLAIN BY

WOUNDS

Wage combat by simultaneously throwing the two dice. If you slay the creature, go to 48. If the creature inflicts a wound on you first, deduct 1 from your STRENGTH RATING and then flee well away from this region by hurrying to 27.

123

The long tunnel at last brings you to the bottom of a huge vertical shaft. The shaft is square-shaped and at each of its four sides sits a crude wooden cage. Your guess is that these cages were used to transport the miners to the top of the shaft. There's a pulley rope attached to each; one end tied to its top and the other end dangling down from the darkness. You wonder which cage you should step into.

If you choose cage on north side	**go to 76**
If you choose cage on south side	**go to 142**
If you choose cage on east side	**go to 178**
If you choose cage on west side	**go to 244**

124

'You're wrong!' the two goblins joyfully respond to your answer. Their fused bodies then leap on to the side of your cage and scamper up to the top. Here they jump up and down with surprising force, causing the cage to twirl. Their next act of mischief, though, is more serious. They reach out for one of the lamps on the wall of the shaft and hold the flame to the rope fastened to the top of the cage. They gleefully jump off as the flame takes. You frantically start heaving on the loose end of the rope again, knowing that you've only a very short while to try and get the cage to the top of the shaft. But the frenzied activity soon tires you out and there's still some metres to go. It looks as if you're not going to make it . . .

Deduct 1 from your STRENGTH RATING. Go next to 247.

You're in luck. It would appear that the creature *is* dead. As you cautiously step right up to it, you find that its bulbous eyes have a fixed gaze. And its hairy limbs are completely rigid. This is a great relief, for there is a huge scimitar in the creature's left claw. When you switch your attention to the diamond, though, there's a flash of light from this scimitar, as if it moved very slightly. You anxiously take another look at the monster. Its eyes don't seem quite as glazed as they were. Is it *really* dead? Or will it suddenly spring to life the moment anyone tries to touch the diamond? You decide to test this,

raising the tip of your sword towards the jewel. This time the creature's whole arm twitches. If you want to make that diamond yours, it's quite clear that you're going to have to fight for it!

If you wish to fight creature   **go to 246**
If you wish to avoid it   **go to 285**

126
As the creature writhes feverishly on the ground there's a hideous rattling of its chain. But the writhing gradually lessens, to be

replaced by an occasional spasm. These then pass too. Certain that it is now dead, you leap over its spread-eagled body and start climbing the rough steps to the top of the pyramid. The huge diamond is almost too big for your haversack but you just manage to squeeze it in. It's also very heavy, making you stagger a little. You're far from complaining, though. A magnificent treasure such as this would be worth a million times the hardship.

Add 1 to the score on your TREASURE COUNTER. Go next to 282.

127

The mountains come nearer and nearer as you follow the rough road, your climb gradually growing steeper and steeper. Finally, as the road turns a sharp corner, you spot a large village ahead. It looks as if it were once thriving, but it now seems almost completely abandoned, an eerie silence hanging over the place. If you did not know otherwise, you would guess that it had been struck by plague. But in a sense it had been – the plague of Draxun's evil. Just behind the village is a sheer crag with a huge man-made hole at its base. This can only be one thing – the thing that the village was so dependent on. The diamond mine! ***Go to 168.***

128

The goblin sniggers again as you try to get back on your feet. You're still very weak and fall back to the ground. 'If you like a risk,' the goblin says, grinning somewhat maliciously, 'then you can perhaps restore the strength that you lost.' He takes out three small phials from the pocket of his shabby jerkin. One contains a blue liquid, one yellow, and one green – but they all have the same strange symbol etched into the glass: ⁖. 'One of these potions will restore some of your strength,' the goblin explains, '. . . and one won't make the slightest bit of difference. As for the third, I'm afraid it will reduce your strength even further!'

If you have found the BOOK OF CIPHERS during your adventure, you may consult it here to find out what the symbol means. This will help you make your choice between the three potions. If you don't possess the BOOK OF CIPHERS, then you'll have to hope for the best in making your decision.

If you choose blue potion	**go to 174**
If you choose yellow potion	**go to 308**
If you choose green potion	**go to 213**

129

'Where are we going?' the husband says, cynically echoing your question. 'Who knows? I *hope* where I can sell my goods. I know that's not much of a hope in this impoverished land, but *anywhere* has to be better than where we've just come from. It used to be the most prosperous community in the kingdom but now it's merely a ghost village!' As he and his wife wearily plod past you, the heavy cart groaning before them, you guess that he must have been referring to the community right next door to the diamond mine. Obviously, the mine had once made it very busy and rich. But now the mine was no longer being worked, the village must have completely lost its custom. *Go to 209.*

130

Although you are knocked unconscious by the fall, it luckily doesn't kill you. When the stars in front of your eyes have disappeared, you look towards that small cave above you again. If there *is* a store of diamonds up there, then you really ought to try one of the other ropes. But what if it *isn't* a store? You would be risking another fall – perhaps a fatal one this time – just for nothing. So you decide to forget about the mysterious hole and continue on your journey through the tunnel. *Go to 33.*

131

The voice tells you that one of the three forks of lightning will restore your strength if you lie directly underneath it. You are wondering *which* fork – the one on the left, the one on the right or the centre – when the next group of flashes illuminate a cryptic carved into the tunnel wall: **X Y X X X Y X**. Does this provide your answer?

If you have picked up the CRYPTICS SCROLL during your adventure, you may consult it here to find out what the cryptic means. If you haven't, you'll have to hope for the best in choosing between the three forks of lightning.

If you choose left	**go to 115**
If you choose right	**go to 233**
If you choose centre	**go to 74**

It isn't very long before you spot your first diamond. You've followed the tunnel for no more than a hundred metres when you pass the entrance to a wide but shallow cave on your right. You're not sure whether this cave has been created by man or nature, but sparkling in the rocky wall at the back of it is the largest and most brilliant diamond you have ever seen. Even in this dim, shadowy light, it seems to shine like ice afire. You're just about to enter the cave, however, when you realise that the jewel has a guardian. Stepping out of the shadows to the diamond's left is the first of Draxun's terrible monsters! *Go to 294.*

You dash through this section of the tunnel, hoping that the roof will hold for just a little longer. But the showers of flint and dust become more and more frequent, heavier and heavier. The creaking is now constant, all around you, becoming an ominous groan. Suddenly, all the stresses and strains prove too much and the roof explodes into an avalanche of rocks and boulders. Fortunately, you're just beyond the main part of the fall but a flying rock strikes you on the back of the head. It leaves you feeling weak and dazed.

Deduct 1 from your STRENGTH RATING. Go next to 92.

You are just beginning to assume that that was the last of the diamonds in this section of the mine when you hear another blood-curdling roar ahead. Your step slows down as tensely you peer into the darkness for a sight of this fiend. For a while there's nothing, but then you make out a black cloak amongst the shadows. That's all there appears to be – just a cloak. For you can detect no face beneath the hood of this cloak and no hands or claws protruding from its sleeves. You wonder if this ghastly being is Death itself; those fears become even greater when it produces a sickle from under its dusty

garment. At last, though, something like a face *does* appear beneath that hood. A semi-decayed skull with two glittering eyes . . .

If you wish to fight creature **go to 105**
If you wish to avoid it **go to 27**

135

'Nidir is not my name,' the old hag tells you. 'Choose again.' You consider the other two possibilities for a moment, finally deciding on Teya. The hag's cackle becomes even more manic than it was before. 'Oh, fool!' she cries with cruel delight. 'I said you were only allowed *one* choice. And that choice was wrong. So you must stay here, prostrate and weak!' But as she and her cackles quickly fade into the darkness, you're determined to defy her. You slice off a handful of your hair with your sword and use it to wipe the slime from your skin. You then haul yourself to your feet. You might not be quite as strong as you were before but you're far from finished yet! **Go to 4.**

136
THIS CREATURE
IS SLAIN BY

WOUNDS

Wage combat by simultaneously throwing the two dice. If you slay the creature, go to 292. If the creature inflicts a wound on you first, deduct 1 from your STRENGTH RATING and then flee well away from this region by hurrying to 12.

137
Turning round again, you gradually approach the spectre hovering in front of you. Your breathing slows almost to a stop as the hazy beckoning finger comes nearer and nearer. You're at last within reach and you shudder as the finger stretches out towards you, pulling you closer. A whisper of a voice emerges from the whitish form, faintly moaning in your ear. 'I am the spectre of Gurvel, an honest miner who used to toil down here,' it wails. 'I was sent to my grave by one of Draxun's monsters. As you have come to defeat these monsters I will try and help. You will see in the wall to your left three loose rocks, one above the other. Behind one is something

that will greatly assist you in your quest. Be sure to choose with care. When one of the rocks has been eased out, the other two will blend back into the wall, becoming impossible to remove.'

If you choose lowest rock	**go to 252**
If you choose middle rock	**go to 41**
If you choose top rock	**go to 172**

138

The canary mysteriously starts to grow. It rapidly gets bigger and bigger, very soon bursting out of its flimsy cage. By now it's huge and it knocks you to the ground, smothering your face with its dense down. You desperately try to push it off but it's far too heavy. You start to suffocate underneath . . .

Deduct 1 from your STRENGTH RATING. Go next to 32.

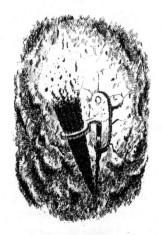

139

You insert your arms into the sleeves of the silk robe and then pull its deep hood over your head. Suddenly you find your hands rising, your fingers pointing towards the sorcerer. His piercing eyes start to fix on those fingers as if he can't avoid them, and there also seems the same lack of control in his voice. 'Yes . . .' he says slowly, vacantly, '. . . you have sent me into a trance. In this state, I or anyone else can be made to say exactly what you want them to say. You can make them tell you what they might not want to tell you; you can make them reveal whether they are truthful or not. This robe will disappear now – and so will I. But the secret of my trance spell will remain with you, to be cast whenever you so desire.'

You may pick up the TRANCE SPELL card. Go next to 99.

140
THIS CREATURE
IS SLAIN BY

WOUNDS

Wage combat by simultaneously throwing the two dice. If you slay the creature, go to 295. If the creature inflicts a wound on you first, deduct 1 from your STRENGTH RATING and then flee well away from this region by hurrying to 12.

141
As you follow the yellow-gowned spirit, the other two suddenly start to snarl and scream after you. 'Don't be troubled by them,' the spirit tells you calmly as she leads you through the very centre of the

cavern. 'They are thus because you chose correctly. But their hatred will soon turn in on itself and destroy them.' Indeed, that seems to be happening because the screams have now turned to terrified howls. You keep your eyes from glancing back as the howls become more and more intense, ending suddenly in sobs – then silence. 'Yes, they have gone,' the spirit ahead tells you. 'And now that I have guided you safely through this treacherous part of the tunnel, I must go to protect any others that might come this way.' And at that, she slowly fades away into the darkness. *Go to 4.*

142

You start pulling on the rope, hauling the cage you have chosen higher and higher up the shaft. Suddenly, however, it stops. You can't shift it a centimetre further. Then two small, flat pebbles suddenly appear on the floor of the cage, one on top of the other. The top pebble has a cipher etched into it: ●. This cipher starts to glow and at the same time manic laughter echoes down the shaft. It's Murgle again. 'You thought it was all going to be so easy, didn't you?' he cries, cackling. 'Well, I have another test for you! One of these two pebbles will make your journey up the shaft much more arduous. I like good sport, though, and so I will give you a chance. You may toss one of the pebbles out of the cage.'

If you have picked up the BOOK OF CIPHERS during your

adventure, you may consult it here to find out if the cipher can help you in making this choice. If not, you'll have to hope for the best.

If you choose top pebble   **go to 165**
If you choose bottom pebble   **go to 324**

143

After you have drunk for a while from the fountain on the right, you wait to see if the deliciously cool water has any effect. But your arms still feel weak, your legs uncertain. So you quickly bend over the other fountain but it disappears back into the ground before you can close your mouth on it. The clone spirit has also disappeared, having apparently vanished into thin air. You rise despairingly to your feet. But at least you *can* get to your feet, so all is not lost. Your strength might not be quite what it was before but it's still enough to enable you to continue with your quest. *Go to 4.*

144

The creature's many eyes are even more hideous in death than they were in life. For as the creature slumps to the ground from your last sword-strike, these eyes start to roll about in their leathery sockets. They all seem to be moving in different directions and several fill with thick red veins. But, at last, one by one the eyes close. When the final eye has shut, the creature's body twitches one more time, and then is still. Now that it is safe to take your horrified gaze from it, you immediately turn your attention to removing the diamond from the rocky wall.

Add 1 to the score on your TREASURE COUNTER. Now hurry well away from this region by going to 12.

The odious creature tries to follow as you move quickly round to the next side of the pyramid. But its sturdy chain suddenly jerks it back. You're very thankful for this – for the second creature's appearance is even more blood-chilling. To fight just one of these demons would be terrifying enough, let alone both together. This creature requires an even sturdier chain and manacle to restrain it. Fanged, dripping jaws snarl rabidly at you, extended so wide that

you can see right to the back of its blood-red throat. There's the same blood-red in its eyes. Surely one of the cruellest, most hostile glares you're ever likely to behold.

If you wish to fight creature	**go to 81**
If you wish to avoid it	**go to 192**

You haven't walked far along the centre of the tunnel when you suddenly trip on a loose rock. As you pick yourself up again, you see that it wasn't a rock at all but a huge diamond! Turning it round in your hands, you wonder why there wasn't a creature guarding it. Suddenly, though, the magnificent jewel turns into a hideous, clinging jelly. You desperately try to get the slime off your fingers but the more you scrape it the more it sticks to you. It now spreads up your arms, starting to cover your whole body. You fall helpless to the ground, writhing within this glutinous cocoon. At last it slides off you, disappearing down a hole in the ground. But how weak has it left you?

Deduct 1 from your STRENGTH RATING. Go next to 328.

147

You hurry further along the tunnel, the creature howling its malevolence at you. To your relief the howls don't get any closer, so the creature obviously isn't catching you up. In fact, you eventually realise that it's not giving chase at all. The howls recede into the darkness behind you. But you soon encounter another creature . . . *Go to 79.*

148

You insert your feet into the sturdy, thick-soled boots. It's your guess that the danger waiting ahead will be something to do with the tunnel floor. Perhaps it will suddenly turn red-hot – or sprout a bed of nails. The danger takes a very different form, though. And your boots are completely useless against it! A piercing wail starts to scream through the tunnel. You immediately clamp your hands to your ears but the sound passes right through them, seeming to penetrate to your very brain. As you drop to your knees in excruciating pain, you can only pray that the hideous noise will soon pass. If it doesn't, it will surely finish you off . . .

Deduct 1 from your STRENGTH RATING. Go next to 15.

149

When you come round again, you find yourself lying on the tunnel floor. The transparent skin all around you has disappeared. You're wondering whether you imagined the bubble when you hear a voice behind you. It's your double again! 'If you take my hand,' he says, offering it to you, 'you will regain all the strength you have lost.' So you reach out for his hand but, just before making contact, you suddenly stop. Is this strange illusion to be trusted?

If you have been taught the TRANCE SPELL, you may cast it here to hypnotise the double into telling you whether he is trying to trick you. To do this, place the TRANCE SPELL CARD exactly over the double's 'mind square' below. If you haven't been taught the TRANCE SPELL, you'll have to hope for the best in deciding whether to trust the double or not.

If you decide to touch him   **go to 302**
If you decide not to touch him   **go to 67**

150

As you follow this left branch of the tunnel, you again find the walls narrowing in on you. Sometimes the distance between them is scarcely more than three metres and your head often grazes the tunnel roof. The intermittent glow from the lamps once more provides almost full illumination. But then, a short distance ahead, you notice an even brighter glow – much brighter, in fact – coming towards you. It's a fireball! You desperately run back down the tunnel to escape it but the fireball hurtles closer and closer. You can soon feel its scorching heat on your back, a heat that quickly saps your strength. Any moment now, you're going to collapse on the ground before it.

Deduct 1 from your STRENGTH RATING. Go next to 35.

151

You choose the white wine thinking it would be more difficult to disguise a potion there. It might make the wine turn cloudy. But who would know with the red or green wine? A short while after draining the horn, though, you feel a strange weakness spreading through your body. Then you hear Murgle's taunting cackle again. So the potion must have been in the white wine after all!

Deduct 1 from your STRENGTH RATING. Go next to 206.

152
THIS CREATURE
IS SLAIN BY

WOUNDS

Wage combat by simultaneously throwing the two dice. If you slay the creature, go to 77. If the creature inflicts a wound on you first, deduct 1 from your STRENGTH RATING and then flee well away from this region by hurrying to 29.

153

You press yourself hard against the tunnel wall, keeping as far away from the whirlwind as possible. Although the wind lashes at your face, you're just able to prevent yourself from being drawn into it. To your horror, though, the whirlwind suddenly starts to move, swirling towards you. It sucks you in as if you are a mere feather, tossing you round and round. You desperately try to break free of its howling grip but your efforts are quite useless against it. Unless the whirlwind subsides very soon, you are surely finished.

Deduct 1 from your STRENGTH RATING. Go next to 307.

154

As soon as you've handed him the diamond, the goblin hides it behind his back. You anxiously wait to see what happens next. Is he going to produce a diamond in both hands for you? Or is he just going to keep your diamond? His expression gives the answer, for an evil-looking smile slowly appears on his face. Realising that you have been tricked, you try and grab hold of the nasty little creature. But his body suddenly turns ice-cold and your fingers freeze on contact. After vigorously blowing on your hands, you try again but this time his body is burning hot. What happens to him next is even more serious. He and your diamond simply dissolve into thin air.

Deduct 1 from the score on your TREASURE COUNTER. Go next to 197.

155

As much as the creature snarls and hisses at you, it refuses to come out of its cave. Perhaps it's concerned about wandering too far from the prize it protects. This also seems to be the concern of the second creature you espy, in the very next cave. It tries to taunt you towards its diamond – a magnificent gemstone glinting white and ice-blue in the cave's rear wall – but it won't desert it. Entranced by this

dazzling specimen, you try to weigh up your chances against the creature. Its only visible weapon is a small dagger, but its slit, fox-like eyes suggest that it has a deadly cunning. Then it bares its teeth in a hideous grin, showing monstrous fangs set in fleshless jaws.

If you wish to fight creature   **go to 90**
If you wish to avoid it   **go to 202**

156

The moment you have picked up the sword, it does exactly as your original one did. It leaps from your hand. But this time it behaves more menacingly. Its blade suddenly turns towards you, slicing the air only centimetres from your face. You quickly raise your shield against it but the swordplay is by far the most deadly you've ever encountered. It swishes through the air at lightning speed and it's all your shield can do to keep up with it . . . *Go to 262.*

157

Suddenly there's another strange sight behind this door. A whirlwind manifests itself there, swirling round fiercely just a few metres in front of you. Concerned that it might suck you in, you step back a pace or two. But you know you must progress beyond it somehow and so you consider the safest way to attempt this. Should you try and pass to its right or left? Or is this whirlwind, too, a bizarre trap . . . and the safest way actually is to walk *straight through its middle*? **Go to 120.**

158

Nabel leads you back to the far side of the cavern. He shows you that it isn't just a solid wall of rock there after all. There's a deep slit in the wall, half-hidden behind a large, upright boulder. Nabel squeezes through this opening. You follow and find yourself in another tunnel! He continues to lead, eventually bringing you to a fork. One branch twists off to the left and the other to the right. ***Go to 103.***

159

'No, we need to go this way!' Lekk calls after you as you head back for the other fork of the tunnel. When he sees that you are ignoring him, he becomes angry. 'All right, don't heed me!' he yells. 'See what will happen to you! The fork you're heading for is full of traps. Don't say I didn't warn you!' You're not sure whether he then continues on his way or starts back for the cavern to rejoin his comrades. The only thing you *are* sure about is that you see no more of him. ***Go to 123.***

160

You hurry after the sound of Gurn's receding footsteps. It's important that you don't let them get too far ahead. You might never find your way back otherwise, for you remember how many times the tunnel from the cavern forked. Soon, however, the faint echo of his footsteps is drowned by a much louder sound. An almighty rumbling starts in the tunnel. Realising that there's about to be a rock-fall, you quickly turn back. You're too late, though. The tunnel roof suddenly collapses. You're buried under a heap of boulders . . .

Deduct 1 from your STRENGTH RATING. Go next to 274.

161

The creature drops to the ground, its mouth a huge, grotesque gape. This time, though, it gapes not in sleep but in death. As soon as you have withdrawn your sword from its crumpled body, you return your attention to the diamond. You warily reach towards it again, waiting for the piercing wail to start. But there's not a sound – even when you have prised the diamond right out of the tunnel wall. In silencing the creature, you obviously silenced the alarm as well.

Add 1 to the score on your TREASURE COUNTER. Now hurry well away from this region by going to 29.

162
THIS CREATURE
IS SLAIN BY

WOUNDS

Wage combat by simultaneously throwing the two dice. If you slay the creature, go to 17. If the creature inflicts a wound on you first, deduct 1 from your STRENGTH RATING and then flee well away from this region by hurrying to 29.

163

Despite your excruciating pain, you think quickly. You have to. 'Don't be a fool, Lekk!' you call. 'If I go down this hole, the diamonds will go with me. I have a haversack full of them. They could all be yours!' For a moment it looks as if your plan won't work. Lekk doesn't seem interested in your offer. Perhaps he has enough diamonds already. Maybe that's how Murgle lured him into his service. Then he starts to pull you slowly up. When you're on firm ground again, you begin to reach into your haversack. But then your fist suddenly flies out, knocking this contemptible being into the hole. When his scream has at last died away, you make your way back to the other, safe, fork of the tunnel. *Go to 123.*

You soon arrive at another of Murgle's petrified creatures. As expected, this too twitches into life when you move a little too close to the diamond. When you step back a couple of paces, it instantly freezes again. You make a close study of the fiend, examining the pair of long, razor-sharp horns jutting out of its forehead, and the

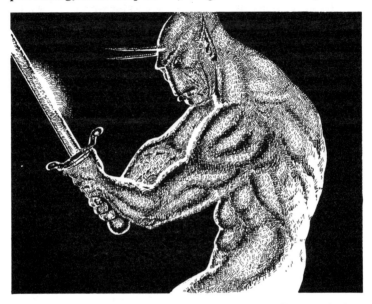

vicious sword it grasps. It looks, unfortunately, as if it would be just as difficult to defeat as the previous three monsters. But how many more diamonds can you hope to come across in this stretch of the tunnel? Perhaps this time you should take a risk with the creature . . .

If you wish to fight creature   **go to 313**
If you wish to avoid it   **go to 29**

You drop the top pebble through the bars of the cage. The moment you hear it hit the ground way below, the cage starts to move upwards again. You pull on the rope once more to help the cage upwards, wondering if you'll hear Murgle's hideous laughter again. Happily, you don't. He clearly isn't pleased with your choice of pebble. ***Go to 247.***

166

'Where am I going? Where there's food and work,' the youth answers in a desperate voice as he turns his hollow eyes to you. 'I was ready to start work in the diamond mine, following in the footsteps of my late father, but then Draxun filled it with his terrible monsters. Now no one dares go down there. A few months back my best friend tried . . . but he hasn't been seen since. The poor fool was obviously overwhelmed by those deadly fiends. At night you can often hear their hideous mocking wails coming from the mine.' Clapping his hands to his ears as if that horrible sound was still echoing there, the youth starts walking slowly again. He looks as if he would like to quicken his pace, get away from the area as swiftly as possible, but his feeble limbs prevent him. ***Go to 209.***

167

There's a huge sparkling diamond at the very top of the pole! You immediately prepare to climb it, removing your sword to make the task a little easier. You've just found your first hand-hold on the broad pole when you suddenly pause. Are the risks even more than they seem? Perhaps some of the monsters will come alive as you reach them. Or – even worse than that – perhaps the pole will suddenly vanish into thin air when you're right at the top. It's then you notice a cryptic chiselled into the wood: **X X Y X Y Y Y**. You're sure that this is telling you whether the pole is safe or not.

If you have picked up the CRYPTICS SCROLL during your adventure, you may consult it here to find out what the cryptic means. If not, you'll have to hope for the best in choosing whether to climb the pole or not.

If you decide to climb pole	**go to 89**
If you decide to ignore it	**go to 114**

168

One or two despairing faces stare at you as you walk through the village. But most of the houses are empty, their doorways and windows filled with silent shadows. You pass a dry village pump, a dusty, abandoned market-place. Starving dogs whine amongst the decaying stalls, searching hopelessly for scraps of food. You're about to toss them a crust of bread from your haversack when you spot a far more deserving recipient; a small child in rags. His eyes are cavernous, distrusting; his body diseased. Unable to bear much more of this, you hurry to the far side of the village, where a short, snaking track leads to the sheer crag . . . and the entrance to the diamond mine. *Go to 75.*

169

You still haven't reached the top of the shaft when your cage comes level with a small cave in the rock. Sitting sideways in this cave, with his knees up, is the strangest goblin you've ever seen. In fact, there are two of them – joined together along the length of their spines.

One faces to the left and one faces to the right. They turn and start to speak to each other over their shoulders. ***Go to 280.***

But are you so fortunate? There is something rather malicious about the goblin's expression. His bulbous eyes seem to twinkle with cruel amusement. He holds a caged canary up to your face. 'There are sometimes dangerous gases in this part of the tunnel,' he tells you. 'Take this canary to give you ample warning of their presence. If the bird dies, you must immediately turn back.' You are not sure whether to trust him, though. His expression still seems cruelly amused. Is it just at the thought of the poor bird losing its life, or is it because the bird constitutes some sort of trap?

*If you have been taught the **TRANCE SPELL** during your adventure, you may cast it here to hypnotise the goblin into telling you whether you should accept the bird. To do this, place the **TRANCE SPELL CARD** exactly over the goblin's 'mind square' below. If you haven't been taught the **TRANCE SPELL**, you'll have to hope for the best in making your decision.*

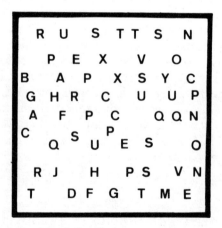

If you decide to take canary	**go to 264**
If you decide to refuse it	**go to 57**

171

You ask the miner why he didn't flee the mine like all the others. He answers that it was a question of pride. 'This mine belongs to Queen Tarsha and her loyal mineworkers,' he says vehemently. 'Not to Draxun and his monsters. They might be able to stop me *working* the mine but they won't ever force me to desert it! I shall stay here until someone comes along to destroy all Draxun's monsters!' When you tell him that that is exactly your mission, the miner immediately takes a scroll from underneath his ragged shirt. 'Then take this!' he insists. 'It explains the cryptics which have been chiselled here and there in the mine. It will help you to avoid many of its dangers!'

You may pick up the CRYPTICS SCROLL. Go next to 33.

172

Having tugged hard at the topmost rock, you eventually pull it free. You expose a small cavity behind it and you eagerly thrust in your hand. There's nothing there – but the cavity seems to go much deeper so you insert your whole arm, right up to the shoulder. You're now touching the very back of the cavity – but you still can't feel anything. You obviously chose the wrong rock. Hurriedly extracting your arm, you try and get a grip on the middle rock before it seals up as the spectre had warned. But it's too quick for you, suddenly melting into the rest of the tunnel wall. The same happens to the rock at the very bottom. It too is now indistinguishable from the rest of the broad rock-face. *Go to 301.*

The creature's frustrated roars echo after you as you hurry further into the tunnel. Again, it has obviously been forbidden to stray from the diamond it protects. You hope that this is also the case with the next fiend you encounter. For this one is quite the most repulsive yet; with maggots writhing from its scalp, cheeks and jaw. Between this mass of maggots are a pair of empty eye sockets and a

set of needle-like fangs. Its warty arms end in claws, the right claw holding a hefty mace. Compared to this abomination, the diamond it protects looks even more beautiful.

If you wish to fight creature	**go to 234**
If you wish to avoid it	**go to 63**

The goblin grins again as you take the phial of blue potion from him and slowly remove the cork. He obviously wants you to hesitate and sweat over your choice but you refuse to give him that pleasure. So you immediately down the liquid in one. The goblin's grin immediately turns into a snarl, not just because you *didn't* agonise over your choice, but because that choice was obviously the correct one. For you can feel the strength rapidly returning to your limbs. The evil little creature flees before you are up on your feet again.

Add 1 to your STRENGTH RATING. Go next to 99.

175
THIS CREATURE
IS SLAIN BY

WOUNDS

Wage combat by simultaneously throwing the two dice. If you slay the creature, go to 82. If the creature inflicts a wound on you first, deduct 1 from your STRENGTH RATING and then flee well away from this region by hurrying to 29.

176
As you're walking along the left side of the ravine, smoke suddenly starts to rise from its depths. This is followed by broad yellow flames, which grow higher and higher. There's now a huge wall of fire between you and the other side of the cavern; the flames so dense that you can't even *see* that other side any more. You back off from the intense heat, keeping as far away from it as possible as you proceed along the tunnel. Fortunately, the tunnel is still very wide. And there's soon a second reason why you are very grateful for this width . . . *Go to 248.*

177
For a long while your passage through this left branch of the tunnel is without incident or obstruction. True, once or twice you think there's a monster lurking at the next bend but then you discover

that it's just the distorted shadows flickering on the rock. Eventually, though, you *do* meet an obstruction. There's a massive pile of rocks just ahead of you, completely blocking your further progress down the tunnel. *Go to 243.*

178

As you start to heave on the rope, the cage rises higher and higher up the shaft. You've hauled yourself some twenty metres from the ground when you see a strange cryptic chiselled into the shaft wall: **XXYXXYY**. You wonder if it is a warning. Perhaps this particular cage is unsafe and the cryptic is warning you not to continue up the shaft. Perhaps you should return to the bottom and use one of the other cages . . .

If you have picked up the CRYPTICS SCROLL during your adventure, you may consult it here to find out what the cryptic means. If not, you'll have to hope for the best in deciding whether to continue or not.

If you choose to continue	**go to 325**
If you choose to return to bottom	**go to 24**

179

Slowly swinging from one hand-hold to another, you carefully make your way along the tunnel wall. You know that just one unsure grip on the jutting rocks will cause you to slide right into the crater. You're now three-quarters of the way along, though, and you're confident that you can make it. But the next protrusion you clasp suddenly comes free from the wall. You're left desperately hanging from one arm. *Go to 223.*

No sooner have you drunk from the fountain on the left than it disappears back into the ground. And that is not the only thing to disappear. When you get up, you see that the clone spirit has vanished into thin air. But all that matters to you is that you are able to stand up with ease again. The strength is rapidly returning to your body. So, making sure you keep well clear of the fungi-covered wall this time, you continue along the tunnel.

Add 1 to your STRENGTH RATING. Go next to 4.

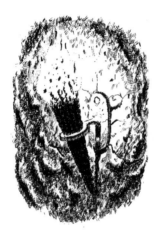

181

You must have ventured into another very rich section of the mine because it's not long before you spot a third diamond in the tunnel wall. This one has worked itself almost completely free of the surrounding rock and you're sure that it would only require a little chipping with your sword to have it in your hand. That's if there weren't a creature snarling just in front of it, of course – a creature that looks even more resilient than the previous two! *Go to 60.*

182

As you reach the top of the rope, just about to lift yourself into the small cave, a face suddenly appears out of the darkness there. It peers at you with frightened but hostile eyes. To begin with, you assume it to be a gnome or a goblin but then you realise that it is much larger than that. It is in fact a man – just an ordinary human being! *Go to 314.*

183

The next creature you encounter down this tunnel is also behind a portcullis and it makes you wonder at the reason for this recurring feature here. Is it because these monsters are *especially* fierce, *especially* difficult to restrain? Would their extreme blood-lust mean that they would otherwise stray from the diamonds? You could certainly believe this of the fiend you're staring at right now. It feverishly shakes the portcullis with huge long-nailed claws. Its snarling face is more like that of a monstrous bat than a human and

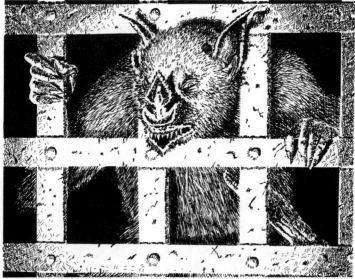

it has a hefty mace hanging from its waist. A direct blow from this cruel, spiked weapon would kill outright. But even a glancing blow would probably seriously injure.

If you wish to fight creature	**go to 162**
If you wish to avoid it	**go to 47**

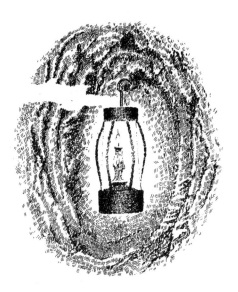

184

You tentatively wade into the pool on the left, the murky water reaching right up to your knees. It's then that the water suddenly starts to bubble and froth. There's much frenzied activity beneath the surface. You're wondering at the cause of this when something tears like a knife into the flesh of your left calf. Then there's a similar ripping and gnawing at your right calf. The water is teaming with piranha fish! As the pool starts to turn red with your blood, you desperately try to reach the other side. Will your badly injured and stumbling legs make it?

Deduct 1 from your STRENGTH RATING. Go next to 112.

185

It seems that the inscription wasn't a warning but an *instruction*. As you pass along the left side of the tunnel, keeping as close to the wall as possible, you discover a diamond there. It's very low down and beyond the glow of the nearest lamp, so you would almost certainly have missed it if you hadn't been on this side. When you have chipped the diamond free from the rock, however, a mysterious laughter echoes through the tunnel. *Go to 290.*

186

The creature proved easier to slay than you expected. Although its
body was powerful, its various hybrid parts made it very unco-
ordinated. With one leg ending in human foot and the other in hoof,
it wasn't able to evade your sword thrusts quickly enough. You
only hope that finding the diamond proves as easy. In your search
for this, you carry one of the lamps right up to the rock just behind
the fallen creature. The diamond immediately twinkles back at
you. It's by no means the largest specimen you've seen in the mine –
but it would probably still fetch a price sufficient to feed half the
kingdom.

*Add 1 to the score on your **TREASURE COUNTER**. Now
hurry well away from this region by going to 281.*

187

'I look the same because I am the same . . .' the three forms all
speak together '. . . although only one of me now embodies the
good spirit. The other two are evil. It is a curse the sorcerer Murgle
put on me to reduce the assistance I can give.' You bewilderedly
turn from one to the other as they all start to beckon you again, each
insisting that she is the one you should trust. For some reason your
gaze again returns to that strange symbol in the centre of their
gowns: ✧.

*If you have picked up the **BOOK OF CIPHERS**, you may
consult it here to find out what the symbol on the gown means.
This will help you make your choice between the three figures. If*

you don't possess the BOOK OF CIPHERS, you'll have to hope for the best in making your decision.

If you choose white figure	**go to 96**
If you choose green figure	**go to 9**
If you choose yellow figure	**go to 141**

188

This creature is much more human in appearance, with hands and feet – but small horns sprout from its elbows and its hairless head is made grotesque by warts. The nose is flat and ape-like and the mouth sports fangs. These fangs show in the monster's hideous smirk as you spot the large diamond in the creature's hand. It taunts

you by repeatedly thrusting this forwards in its open palm. You haven't failed to notice what is in the creature's other hand, though, the one it hides behind its back. A huge studded club!

If you wish to fight creature	**go to 270**
If you wish to avoid it	**go to 5**

THIS CREATURE
IS SLAIN BY

WOUNDS

Wage combat by simultaneously throwing the two dice. If you slay the creature, go to 161. If the creature inflicts a wound on you first, deduct 1 from your STRENGTH RATING and then flee well away from this region by hurrying to 29.

190
Hoping that your fingers can hold on just long enough, you start to swing your body from side to side, making each swing take you nearer and nearer to the other side of the crater. When you've swung as far out as you think you can, you suddenly release your grip on the rock and throw your body across the gap. You put every last bit of strength into your leap. Although you land awkwardly, you just about make it! ***Go to 239.***

191
You've clambered about three-quarters of the way up the statue – at least fifteen metres from the ground – when it suddenly starts to vibrate. You desperately cling on to it, hoping that the vibration will soon pass. But it only increases . . . and then something even worse happens. The statue starts to dissolve! You frantically try to make your way down again while there's still something to hold on to but the stone becomes more and more elusive. Suddenly it has gone altogether and you plunge screaming towards the tunnel floor way, way below. You lie there unconscious . . . or is it even worse than that?

Deduct 1 from your STRENGTH RATING. Go next to 249.

You hurry round to this last side of the pyramid because you can't believe that a third creature could be quite as horrific. Unfortunately, you are wrong. This monster guardian is equally terrifying. Its whole skeleton is made up of bony lumps, these lumps sometimes even breaking through the warty, green skin. In each of its cavernous eye sockets it has not one eyeball, but two, and these

twin red glares burn into you like flaming coals. In its foaming mouth is a complex set of tusks; long thin ones protruding from the lower jaw and shorter but much thicker ones protruding from the upper. As if these natural weapons weren't enough, it also clenches a huge sword in its left claw.

If you wish to fight creature	**go to 256**
If you wish to avoid it	**go to 282**

You haven't followed the dim, twisting glow of this middle tunnel very far when you suddenly hear a loud growling ahead. You freeze in your tracks, wondering whether to turn back. Although that sound almost certainly means there is a diamond near, you are concerned at how narrow this tunnel is. If you choose not to fight the creature, there would be little room to slip past it. You then realise that the deep sound is not growling but *snoring*. It might belong to a monster, but at least that monster is asleep! So you very quietly continue forwards . . . ***Go to 311.***

194

There's suddenly a massive rock-fall in the tunnel you came by, completely sealing off its entrance! And then, moments later, you hear a crashing of rock and the same thing happens in the other two tunnels. All three routes are now completely blocked! You drop to your knees in despair, realising that Murgle has beaten you. You have no doubt that the rock-falls *were* his evil doing. You clamp your hands to your ears as you hear a voice start to speak. This must be the gloating sorcerer. But then you realise that the voice is not coming from way above but from only just behind you. And that it's an ordinary, human voice . . . ***Go to 69.***

195

The puff of white smoke proves much denser than it looked. You'd thought that a couple of steps would take you right through it, to the other side. But it's as if you have entered an endless fog. As you wade through these swirling vapours, your ears can just detect the gnome's cackle again. It's proof that you chose the *wrong* puff of smoke! Finally, you emerge from it but – strangely – you find yourself standing in exactly the same part of the tunnel as you were before. YOU, though, are not exactly the same as before. That smoke seems to have sapped much of your strength . . .

Deduct 1 from your STRENGTH RATING. Go next to 197.

196

'Long ago,' the miner tells you in a slow, whispery voice, 'I too was buried under a rock-fall. I wasn't as lucky as you, however. I didn't survive. But do not grieve for me. My spirit returns to help mortals such as yourself . . .' Suddenly, three iron goblets appear on the ground beside you. Each has a thick white vapour steaming round its rim and is engraved with a strange cipher: ✳. 'One of these three potions can restore the strength you have lost,' the spirit explains. 'You must guess which, though, and you're permitted only one guess. Good luck. I must immediately take my leave of you.'

If you have picked up the BOOK OF CIPHERS during your adventure, you may consult it here to find out what the cipher means. If not, you'll have to hope for the best in making your choice between the three goblets.

If you choose left goblet	**go to 80**
If you choose middle goblet	**go to 309**
If you choose right goblet	**go to 30**

197

Suddenly everything becomes pitch-dark. Then you hear a small creak in front of you. It's the creaking of a heavy wooden door. You seem to have arrived at another one. Stepping through it, you are immediately greeted by Murgle's manic laughter again. It's exactly the same as it was before and you wonder if everything that happened since then really happened at all. 'So how did you like my mind maze?' the sorcerer asks with a nasty cackle, his evil face floating above you once more. 'It has left you very confused, has it not? But all that need matter to you is that you survived it. Yes, you have survived another of my trials! I wonder how you will fare, though, in the next part of the mine? For this is the most perilous of all!' *Go to 235.*

198

You slowly make your way beyond the site of the rock-fall. Again, several times, you think that there's a creature lurking at a distant bend. But again it's merely the dancing shadows. Just as you start to relax, however, a bend *does* suddenly produce a creature. It leaps out at you from the shadows. Fortunately, though, it's just a small goblin. *Go to 170.*

199

You keep pulling very slowly on the rope. The cage hasn't climbed much further, however, when there's another disconcerting jolt. A second strand of the rope must have given way. You hold your breath, hoping there isn't much further to go. You give the rope the gentlest of tugs that you can. But then the rope above you snaps completely and the cage plunges down the shaft. The flimsy construction shatters as soon as it hits the ground, leaving your body lifeless amongst the debris. Have you just been knocked unconscious, or is it much worse than that?

Deduct 1 from your STRENGTH RATING. Go next to 55.

200
THIS CREATURE
IS SLAIN BY

WOUNDS

Wage combat by simultaneously throwing the two dice. If you slay the creature, go to 161. If the creature inflicts a wound on you first, deduct 1 from your STRENGTH RATING and then flee well away from this region by hurrying to 29.

201
The rope is now pulling against you so hard that it's burning your hands. You have no choice but to let go and you cringe, terrified, in the cage as it plummets towards the iron spikes. Any second now you'll be impaled on them! But within just centimetres of the

spikes, however, the cage suddenly stops. This is obviously Murgle's cruel sense of humour at work. When you try pulling on the rope again, you find that it isn't quite so resistant. So you slowly make your way up the shaft once more. ***Go to 169.***

Go to 169.

202

The next cave your gaze turns to is without a creature – and so also, you assume, without a diamond. But the one after that, the last of the caves round this huge cavern, reverberates with the furious roar of a shaven-headed brute. Its powerful forearms are encased in spiked armlets and it wields a horrific-looking mace around its

glistening body. The weapon's hissing arc almost completely fills the cave, occasionally grazing its rough sides. You wonder if there would be just enough room for you to manoeuvre in there; just enough room for you to be able to defeat the creature. For although you haven't spotted it yet, surely only the presence of a priceless jewel would explain such a fearsome guard?

If you wish to fight creature	**go to 2**
If you wish to avoid it	**go to 289**

203

You sit on the grass at the edge of the road, resting your back against a large rock. While you are resting, a group of ragged people approach from the direction of the mine. They tramp the hard road with bare feet, eyes dejectedly turned towards the ground. There are five of them in all: at the front a bearded man with a rusty pickaxe over his shoulder; some distance behind him a scrawny youth; then an old man with long, filthy hair; and bringing up the rear a sad-faced husband and wife pushing a cart full of earthenware pots. Curious to know where they are going, you decide to speak to one of them as they pass. Who will you choose?

If bearded man	**go to 86**
If youth	**go to 166**
If old man	**go to 38**
If husband and wife	**go to 129**

204

As you wait, the falls of flint and dust ahead of you become thicker and thicker, more and more frequent. To your concern, they also start to come nearer, eventually showering down on to your shoulders and hitting your back. The creaking becomes more and more strained and you've absolutely no doubt now that a rock-fall will have to occur to relieve these stresses. Suddenly, it happens – rocks and boulders crashing down from the tunnel roof. But, fortunately, it's at least thirty metres in front of you and you're just out of range of the flying debris. And, just as fortunately, the rubble – once it has settled – isn't so deep as to obstruct your progress. You manage to scramble over the top of it and continue your journey through the tunnel. *Go to 92.*

205

You insert your arms into the sleeves of the velvet robe and then pull its deep hood over your head. Velvet seems the most likely material in which to learn a sorcerer's magic and you are convinced that you chose correctly. But as you loosely knot the tasselled rope round the garment, you notice the sorcerer start to dissolve into the shadowy air. He sadly shakes his head as he does so. Realising that your choice must have been wrong, you quickly throw off the velvet robe and try to grab one of the others on his arm. But they, too, are rapidly fading and your hand is just too late. *Go to 99.*

206

'Ah, so you have managed to come through *that* trial as well!' the evil sorcerer observes casually. 'It matters little. There will be many more for you before you reach the exit from the mine. I could, of course, just destroy you right now. One bolt from my fingertips and you would be finished. But I might as well enjoy watching your struggles for a while. I have little else to amuse me. I think we'll next try the mind maze.' And at that the sorcerer slowly raises his right hand . . . *Go to 22.*

207
THIS CREATURE
IS SLAIN BY

WOUNDS

Wage combat by simultaneously throwing the two dice. If you slay the creature, go to 40. If the creature inflicts a wound on you first, deduct 1 from your STRENGTH RATING and then flee weil away from this region by hurrying to 5.

208
Lekk continues to lead you through the tunnel. Eventually, it forks. One fork leads off to the left and the other to the right. 'We need to follow the fork to the right,' he tells you and he steps back to allow you to go first. This you do but after a few steps you become

suspicious. Why has he suddenly let you take the lead? You wonder whether it's a trap, whether you should have really followed the other fork . . .

If you have been taught the TRANCE SPELL during your adventure, you may cast it here to find out whether Lekk is telling the truth or not. To do this, place the TRANCE SPELL CARD exactly over his 'mind square' below. If you haven't been taught the TRANCE SPELL, you'll have to hope for the best in deciding what to do.

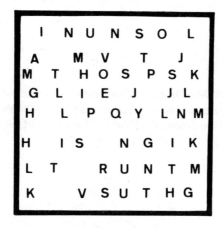

```
I   N  U  N  S  O  L
A     M  V  T     J
M  T  H  O  S  P  S  K
 G  L  I  E  J     J  L
 H     L  P  Q  Y  L  N  M
H    I  S     N  G  I  K
L  T        R  U  N  T  M
K        V  S  U  T  H  G
```

If you decide to continue along right fork	**go to 237**
If you decide to return to left fork	**go to 159**

209

When you have watched the ragged group slowly disappear into the
distance, you decide that it's time for you to start moving again. On
your way towards the mine, you pass a few more wretched figures.
Their dejected faces don't once look up at you, little realising that
you could be their saviour. The rough road becomes steeper and
steeper, the mountain-tops growing clearer and clearer. Turning a
sharp bend, you suddenly spot a large village ahead, at the base of a
sheer crag. The place is almost completely deserted, an eerie silence
hanging over it. But it's not the village that holds your gaze – it's a
huge man-made hole in that crag. It must be the diamond mine!
Go to 168.

210

The creature's hideous smirk is no more as your second sword-
thrust runs clean through its body. Yes, it was very cunning – but
you proved even more so, cleverly out-manoeuvring it in the
combat. Triumphant, you step over the crumpled body of the
fiend, making towards your prize at the back of the cave. The
diamond, though three-quarters exposed, is set very firmly in its
rocky surround and you decide to use the creature's dagger to chip
it free. You don't want to risk using your own weapon in case you
snap it.

*Add 1 to the score on your TREASURE COUNTER. Now
hurry well away from this cavern by fleeing to 289.*

You can now see that the creature's chain is of huge iron links, secured round one of its scaly ankles. The chain limits its movement to just this side of the pyramid but it is not so short as to

restrict its manœuvrability in a fight. So you should be aware of the full dangers involved in taking on this hideous creature. Do you consider yourself a worthy match for those flailing, vicious claws and that hefty sword it carries?

If you wish to fight creature   **go to 329**
If you wish to avoid it   **go to 145**

212
Your heart almost stopped, you answer the beckoning finger of the spectre behind, slowly stepping towards the hazy form. The face is no more than curling white wisps, like twists of smoke from a group of candles, and it is impossible to tell whether the expression is hostile or not. But just after its transparent fingers have icily touched your shoulder, the expressionless face emits a hideous

laugh. A moment later, it brings its hazy pickaxe crashing down on your skull. If it had been a real pickaxe it would, of course, have killed you. But even this ethereal one somehow still knocks you to the ground. When you eventually rise to your feet again, dazed and groggy, the spectre is gone.

Deduct 1 from your STRENGTH RATING. Go next to 301.

213

The goblin's malicious little grin broadens as you take the phial of green potion from him and remove the cork. Does that mean that you made the wrong choice – or simply that he's trying to make you *think* that you made the wrong choice? You're convinced that it's just the latter so you quickly swallow the potion. Unfortunately, you are wrong! The goblin's sudden cackling tells you this, and a strange haziness now fills your head. You desperately reach out towards the goblin, trying to snatch one of the other phials from him, but your arm drops listlessly to your side . . .

Deduct 1 from your STRENGTH RATING. Go next to 254.

214

The sorcerer's laughter suddenly switches to an incensed roar. 'But don't think that your luck will continue!' he screams at you, the manic eyes seeming to burn right into your very soul. 'Draxun has threatened me with death on the rack should anyone leave this mine. So I have many more trials for you! The first of these is right now . . .' ***Go to 42.***

There's something rather sinister-looking about the pools, though. A thin mist hovers over each murky surface. You therefore start to wonder if one or maybe even two of the pools is a trap.

*If you have acquired the **POWER OF FORESIGHT** during your adventure, you may employ it here to find out which of these pools should be avoided. To do this, place the **FORE-SIGHT POWER CARD** exactly over the 'eye' shape below. If you haven't acquired the **POWER OF FORESIGHT**, you'll have to hope for the best in choosing which pool to wade through.*

If you choose left pool	**go to 184**
If you choose middle pool	**go to 106**
If you choose right pool	**go to 13**

Then you feel the sucking at your arm; at your thigh. There are dozens of evil-looking fungi growing along this rock-face, each with a powerful sucker. They're attaching themselves all over the right side of your body, pulling at your flesh, seeming to draw all the strength out of you. You're like a fly caught in a Venus's fly-trap. Thrashing about in vain, you feel yourself growing weaker and weaker . . .

Deduct 1 from your STRENGTH RATING. Go next to 317.

217

As you climb the rope on the left, you hear a light tinkling above you. It's only when you've nearly reached the top that you suddenly realise that the tinkling is caused by your movement up the rope. There must be a small bell attached to the rope. That bell can only have one purpose – to give warning that the rope is being used! Greatly alarmed by this, you quickly start to descend again. But it's too late. Someone in the cave suddenly cuts the rope above you and you go crashing to the hard ground below . . .

Deduct 1 from your STRENGTH RATING. Go next to 130.

218
THIS CREATURE
IS SLAIN BY

WOUNDS

Wage combat by simultaneously throwing the two dice. If you slay the creature, go to 101. If the creature inflicts a wound on you first, deduct 1 from your STRENGTH RATING and then flee well away from this region by hurrying to 12.

You jump back from the flying splinters of ice as the creature crashes to the ground. To your surprise and horror, it is not water that spills from its many wounds but blood. Blood as red and sticky as any human's! You're so mesmerised by this that for a while you completely forget your reason for fighting the monster. But then you remember the diamond and start to search for it in the tunnel wall. There seems to be nothing there, though, but the coarse, black rock. Despondent, you're just about to give up when you notice that the ice-creature's left claw is holding something. The reason you hadn't noticed it before is because the object is of exactly the same bluish white as the creature. It's the diamond!

Add 1 to the score on your TREASURE COUNTER. Now hurry well away from this region by going to 12.

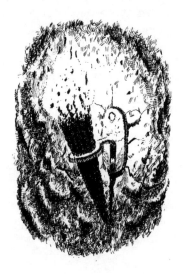

220

The next creature you encounter – another five hundred metres or so along the massive tunnel – isn't quite as large but, quite unbelievably, it is even *more* grotesque. Again, the nearby flames accentuate this ugliness, gouging red and black shadows into the creature's wart-ridden face. Its flared nostrils are cavernous with these shadows, as are its leathery cheeks. The warts continue all the way down the creature's muscular arms to a pair of clawed hands.

The left of these grips a barbed, curved sword. This, too, flashes with red reflection and your spine chills as you consider how there might soon be another red there; the red of your blood. But it is not just this sword that is reddened by the flames. Twinkling like a ruby is the diamond that the fiend is guarding. Can you possibly resist it?

If you wish to fight creature   **go to 44**
If you wish to avoid it   **go to 116**

221

You have walked much further down this branch of the tunnel when you come across three items of miner's clothing on the tunnel floor. They are a pair of sturdy leather boots, an iron helmet and a pair of earmuffs fashioned from wood and animal fur. You're wondering what they are doing there when there's a flash of green light right in front of you and a wizard appears. ***Go to 23.***

222

Far from being cursed, you find that the shovel you have chosen is magic! You're just about to slide it under some of the rocks when it suddenly leaps from your hands. It then starts to do the digging of its own accord! You watch amazed as it works through the pile of rocks a hundred times faster than you could have done. Within minutes it has moved enough of them to one side to open up a channel through the massive heap. It's just wide enough for you to squeeze through. *Go to 198.*

223

The strain on that one arm still holding on to the rock is immense. It has your whole body weight to support. You can feel the muscles rapidly growing weaker and weaker. Any moment now your fingers are surely going to lose their grip. Since you are in much too awkward a position to try and make your way back again, it seems that you have only one chance. That is to swing your body again and try and jump the rest of the way to the other side of the crater. If you make it, then you will be left with no more than badly-strained arm muscles. If you don't, of course, then the result is likely to be much worse than that . . .

Deduct 1 from your STRENGTH RATING. Go next to 190.

224

Your eyes eventually open again but you can still only see a blur in front of you. Then you see a hideous face cackling in this blur. Your eyes slowly focus on the spirit, who now has the leathery, wrinkled features of an old woman. 'I am Murgle's creation,' she says, cackling at you. 'And I have led you into my trap. But I always like to play fair with my victims. You can restore the strength that the slime has taken from you if you can guess my name. Is it Nidir, Teya or Kadris? You have only one chance.'

If you have been taught the TRANCE SPELL during your adventure, you may cast it here to make the spirit reveal her correct name. To do this, place the TRANCE SPELL CARD exactly over her 'mind square' below. If you haven't been taught the TRANCE SPELL, you'll have to hope for the best in making your decision.

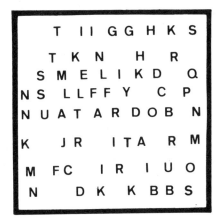

If you choose Nidir	**go to 135**
If you choose Teya	**go to 320**
If you choose Kadris	**go to 49**

You haven't walked far along the right side of the ravine when flames appear from its depths. They grow higher and higher, soon forming a dense wall of fire between the two sides of the cavern. It is impossible to cross the ravine now! The intense heat forces you to keep as close to the side of the tunnel as possible. After three or four hundred metres, though, you suddenly have to move away from it again. There's a scaly, multi-eyed creature standing there, dribbling yellow slime from its fangs . . . *Go to 97.*

226
THIS CREATURE
IS SLAIN BY

WOUNDS

Wage combat by simultaneously throwing the two dice. If you slay the creature, go to 144. If the creature inflicts a wound on you first, deduct 1 from your STRENGTH RATING and then flee well away from this region by hurrying to 12.

227

As soon as you touch the white sword, its glow disappears and its colour returns to the dull grey it was before. Your sword is of iron again and you gratefully put it in its sheath. You wonder what would have happened if you had picked up one of the other two swords. Perhaps they would have retained their mystical glow and been much more potent weapons. But perhaps they would have simply vanished as soon as your hand made contact and you would have been left weaponless. *Go to 197.*

228

You have followed the middle branch for quite a way when the lamp just ahead of you starts to flicker erratically. For a terrifying moment you wonder whether this and all the other lamps are about to go out, leaving you in complete darkness. Something very different happens, though. The wafts of blue and amber smoke from the flickering lamp collect together into the shape of a strange figure. He is like an Oriental slave; with a shaved head and bracelets of iron on his huge, folded arms. A gold tooth shows as he starts to speak . . . *Go to 326.*

229

The third diamond you come across in this tunnel – another four or five hundred metres further along – is also protected by only a sleeping creature. By now, though, you're not in any way duped by this. You know that you can creep past the creature – perhaps even give it a prod – and it will continue to snore. But should you make the slightest movement towards the diamond, Murgle's magic has seen to it that the creature will immediately be jolted out of its sleep.

And what a terrifying thing that would be in this case. Although squat, the creature looks unbelievably strong. Its arms and legs have the gnarled texture of tree bark and they seem to be almost as

thick as tree-trunks, too. There's a razor-sharp spear lying across its massive chest. Just a glancing blow with this would surely cause serious injury. But then your eye strays back to that magnificent diamond . . .

If you wish to fight creature   **go to 68**
If you wish to avoid it   **go to 268**

230

You were wise to decide not to try and climb the statue, for a few minutes later it suddenly disappears. You could have been left there in mid-air, some ten or fifteen metres from the ground. The fall might well have killed you. So you resolve only to be tempted by diamonds found in the tunnel wall from now on. Although they always seem to have a vicious monster to guard them, at least you can be sure that they are real! *Go to 157.*

You jab your sword into the bubble, expecting it to burst and disappear. But you merely make a small hole in it. You realise that you're going to have to slice its tough skin right open, from top to bottom. When the cut seems wide enough, you step into the bubble yourself so you can drag out the trapped double. The moment you are inside, though, the cut immediately seals up again. You are now trapped yourself! You desperately start hacking at the bubble again, but its skin seems even tougher on the inside and your sword makes not the slightest impression. All this frenzied activity quickly uses up the remaining air as well and you soon pass out . . .

Deduct 1 from your STRENGTH RATING. Go next to 149.

232

'You took a diamond from the top of the pole, did you not?' the goblin asks. 'Don't look so wary. I've not come to accuse you of theft. Indeed, I've come to double your riches. Just hand me that one diamond and I will give you back *two*!' Your wariness remains, however. The goblin's voice is just as strange and changeable as his colour. One moment it is a snigger, the next very solemn . . . You're really not sure whether you should trust him or not.

If you have been taught the TRANCE SPELL during your adventure, you may cast it here to hypnotise the goblin into telling you if he is honest. To do this, place the TRANCE SPELL CARD exactly over the goblin's 'mind square' below. If you haven't been taught the TRANCE SPELL, you'll have to hope for the best in choosing whether to hand over the diamond or not.

If you decide to hand it over   **go to 154**
If you refuse to hand it over   **go to 21**

233

Crawling towards the right side of the tunnel, you wait for the next fork of lightning to strike there. When it does, it passes right through your body, sending you into a wild spasm. You're certain that this is the end of you! But the spasm leaves you feeling surprisingly invigorated. And when you look down at your injuries, caused by the explosion, you find that they have completely disappeared. You rise happily to your feet.

Add 1 to your STRENGTH RATING. Go next to 197.

234
THIS CREATURE
IS SLAIN BY

WOUNDS

Wage combat by simultaneously throwing the two dice. If you slay the creature, go to 299. If the creature inflicts a wound on you first, deduct 1 from your STRENGTH RATING and then flee well away from this region by hurrying to 281.

235

Again Murgle suddenly disappears and you're left to reflect on his warning. *The next part of the mine is the most perilous of all!* You wonder *why* it is so perilous. Are there even fiercer creatures in the tunnels ahead, traps even more deadly? You shudder at the idea, proceeding even more nervously than you did before. You haven't gone very far when the cavern branches into three much smaller tunnels. Which should you follow?

If you choose left tunnel	**go to 66**
If you choose right tunnel	**go to 277**
If you choose middle tunnel	**go to 193**

236

This branch of the tunnel seems to go on and on, twisting to left and right through the darkness. Suddenly, out of this darkness there looms the head of a grotesque monster. Or is it a monster – for the head is completely motionless. Cautiously approaching it, you find that it is just a gargoyle-like face chiselled into the tunnel wall, presumably the work of the miners. Examining the hideous carving more closely, you see that there is a strange inscription beneath it: **XYYXXYX**. You wonder if this cryptic inscription gives some sort of instruction.

If you have picked up the CRYPTICS SCROLL during your adventure, you may consult it here to find out what the inscription means. If you haven't, you'll have to guess the meaning.

If you think it means	
KEEP TO LEFT	**go to 296**
If you think it means	
KEEP TO CENTRE	**go to 146**
If you think it means	
KEEP TO RIGHT	**go to 328**

237

You dismiss your suspicious thoughts, feeling guilty about having them. Lekk probably just wants you to go first because you are armed. He's perhaps afraid that there might be monsters down the tunnel. You haven't ventured much further, however, when the tunnel floor suddenly gives way beneath you. It's a concealed pothole! Fortunately, you manage to grab hold of the edge at the very last moment. It's only your fingertips, though, that stop you dropping into the depths . . . ***Go to 306.***

238

The sound is a spine-chilling roar. And this time, unfortunately, you *are* able to see where the sound is coming from. There's a grotesque hybrid creature further along the tunnel. Its mutant face has the horns of a ram but the nose and small tusks of a hog. A spiny

fin runs down its head. Its hybrid characteristics continue in its body; the left arm being that of a man and the right being that of a gorilla. It is this arm which holds the creature's weapon; a vicious, coarse-toothed scimitar.

If you wish to fight creature	**go to 51**
If you wish to avoid it	**go to 173**

As you continue beyond the crater, the tunnel grows even wider. It's now more like a small cavern than a tunnel. Fortunately, the lamps are placed more frequently here and so your way ahead is not quite as uncertain as it might have been. But there are still many more pockets of darkness than light and it is in one of these dark areas that you suddenly catch sight of a huge, glinting diamond in the rock-face. But as you move nearer, however, you see that there is also a monster with two heads nearby. Both of its mouths hiss at you with snake-like tongues, each dripping a luminous venom. By

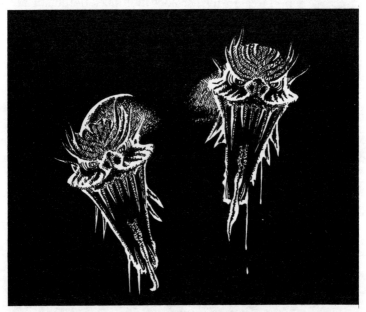

now you've worked out that these monster-guardians never desert the diamonds they protect. Indeed, it seems that they are unable to move more than a couple of paces from them. So, by keeping to the other side of the tunnel, you're sure you could happily avoid this fiend. But do you really want to? For that diamond glinting in the rock is the largest you've seen yet . . .

If you wish to fight creature   **go to 283**
If you wish to avoid it   **go to 10**

240

You have continued only a short way further along the tunnel when you hear a terrifying crash echoing behind you. It sounds like another rock-fall. It's fortunate that you didn't try and make your way back after all. You would have been crushed to death. As you press forwards, however, you feel as much sorrow as relief. *You* might have escaped that terrible fate but you're sure Gurn couldn't have. By your calculation, he would have been exactly in the middle of the fall. You now feel especially bad about not totally trusting him. *Go to 123.*

241
THIS CREATURE
IS SLAIN BY

WOUNDS

Wage combat by simultaneously throwing the two dice. If you slay the creature, go to 273. If the creature inflicts a wound on you first, deduct 1 from your STRENGTH RATING and then flee well away from this region by hurrying to 29.

242

As you catch up with Nabel in this right branch of the tunnel, he notices the suspicious sideways look you keep giving him. He smiles knowingly. 'Ah, so you've seen a mirage of me!' he exclaims. 'Or are you wondering if *I* am the mirage. That's Murgle up to his evil magic again, I'm afraid. He creates mirages from time to time to lure the unsuspecting into traps. It's a good thing you followed the real me. That other branch of the tunnel is riddled with traps. But we must make sure Murgle doesn't try that trick on you again. The only way to be sure is if I take my leave of you here. Anyway, your route is straightforward from now on.' *Go to 123.*

243

This rock-fall had obviously been fatal because you discover several skeletons under the rubble. But there's also something amongst the grisly bones that cheers you; three shovels! They must have belonged to the miners killed by the rock-fall. Tugging them out and propping them up against the tunnel wall, you notice that they all have the same strange symbol chiselled into their handles: ※. This starts to make you feel uneasy. Does it mean that one or more of them is cursed in some way and will harm you if you try to use it to clear a path? You had better select your shovel with care!

If you have picked up the BOOK OF CIPHERS during your adventure, you may consult it here to find out which shovel to use. If not, you'll have to hope for the best in making your decision.

If you choose left shovel	**go to 222**
If you choose middle shovel	**go to 104**
If you choose right shovel	**go to 50**

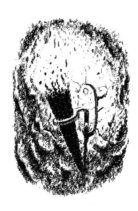

244

The cage starts to rise up the shaft as you pull on the loose rope. You've ascended some twenty metres or so when you notice a message scrawled on the floor of the cage. It reads: *One side of this floor is unsafe. Be sure to keep to the other side.* But *which* is the unsafe side? The message doesn't say. There is a cryptic scrawled beneath the message, however: **XXYXYYX**. You're sure that *this* gives you the answer you're looking for.

*If you have picked up the **CRYPTICS SCROLL** during your adventure, you may consult it here to find out what the cryptic means. If not, you'll have to hope for the best in deciding on which side of the cage floor to stand.*

If you choose left side	**go to 312**
If you choose right side	**go to 118**

245

You desperately try to prevent the cage's determined descent, pulling for all you are worth on the rope. But it's as much as you can do to keep the cage stationary, let alone make it climb again. Even this surely can't last for long. Any moment now your exhausted arms are going to have to let go . . .

Deduct 1 from your STRENGTH RATING. Go next to 201.

246
THIS CREATURE
IS SLAIN BY

WOUNDS

Wage combat by simultaneously throwing the two dice. If you slay the creature, go to 82. If the creature inflicts a wound on you first, deduct 1 from your STRENGTH RATING and then flee well away from this region by hurrying to 29.

247

Having finally reached the top of the shaft, you quickly step out of the cage. Your heart leaps with joy as you spot the most wonderful sight ahead. Daylight! But it's just a pin-prick, still some distance away. You've got to pass through one more long, shadowy cavern. The cavern is not completely dark, though, for there's a strange blue-white glow at its very centre. It becomes stronger as you approach. You suddenly stop dead in your tracks, gaping in wonder. You can now see what causes the glow. Sitting atop a stone pyramid is a diamond so large that it makes all the others you've seen seem like mere pebbles! *Go to 83.*

A blood-red fiend suddenly steps out in front of you! Its eagle-like claws slash the air only centimetres from your face. You dart as close to the wall of fire as you can bear, hoping the creature won't do

likewise. To your great relief, it doesn't. It's either the heat that deters it or fear of Murgle's wrath. So you could now easily continue past the creature . . . but then you notice the glittering diamond in the rock behind it.

> If you wish to fight creature   **go to 136**
> If you wish to avoid it   **go to 39**

You slowly come round, stars before your eyes. When they are finally able to focus you see that the statue has vanished. Or was it never really there? The tunnel roof is surely no more than four or five metres above you, so how could such a gigantic statue have possibly fitted there? But then you have another strange experience on this side of the oak door. For, out of the darkness, a floating, luminous skull suddenly approaches you. *Go to 14.*

250
THIS CREATURE
IS SLAIN BY

WOUNDS

Wage combat by simultaneously throwing the two dice. If you slay the creature, go to 161. If the creature inflicts a wound on you first, deduct 1 from your STRENGTH RATING and then flee well away from this region by hurrying to 29.

251

As you start to climb down the series of rungs, you realise how busy the mine must have once been. The rungs are very shiny, worn from frequent use. You wonder how many miners climbed up and down them per day. Fifty? A hundred? And that was just *this* series of rungs, of course. There would have been the same number of men using those on the other side of the hole. Because the rungs are so shiny, you are very careful as you lower yourself from one to the other. What makes your task even more difficult is that there are no lamps on the way down. You only hope that the trail of lamps starts again as soon as you reach the bottom of the shaft. But *when* will you reach the bottom? The rungs seem to go on for ever. You have counted more than four hundred now. At last, though, your lower foot touches firm ground. *Go to 91.*

You tensely ease out the lowest rock, your fingertips just able to secure a grip on it. There's a narrow but deep cavity behind it and you immediately insert your arm. To begin with you are disappointed but, as your arm disappears right up to the shoulder, your fingers suddenly touch something of grained leather. It's the cover of a thick book. Sliding the book out, you see that it is very decayed; the pages crumbling and yellow. But you can still just about make out the crude lettering on these pages and the strange drawings alongside. You assume these drawings to be various ciphers employed in the mine, and you therefore carefully place the book into your haversack.

You may pick up the BOOK OF CIPHERS card. Go next to 301.

253

Horrified, you continue to stare at the three giant bubbles. Inside each bubble your double is desperately trying to claw himself free. The bubbles' skin must be tougher than it looks. Unable to bear this terrible sight any longer, you immediately draw your sword to cut your doubles free. But for some reason you suddenly have this feeling that you should only go to the rescue of _one_ of the doubles. The other two bubbles are there merely as traps!

If you have acquired the POWER OF FORESIGHT during your adventure, you may employ it here to find out which of the bubbles are traps. To do this, place the FORESIGHT POWER

CARD exactly over the 'eye' shape below. If you haven't acquired the *POWER OF FORESIGHT*, you'll have to hope for the best in choosing which bubble to cut.

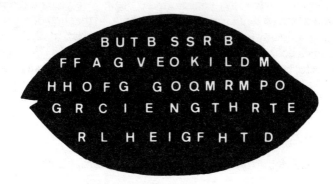

BUT B SSR B
FF A G V E O K I L D M
HH O F G   G O Q M R M P O
G R C I E N G T H R T E
R L H E I G F H T D

If you decide on left bubble   **go to 231**
If you decide on middle bubble   **go to 304**
If you decide on right bubble   **go to 37**

254

By the time you have recovered enough to continue your exploration of the mine the goblin has gone. He seems to have scurried off into the darkness. You wonder if that is the echo of his cackle you can just hear in the distance. Or is it just a trick played on your hearing: not really belonging to anything at all. *Go to 99.*

255

As soon as you enter the puff of blue smoke, you hear the gnome's cackle again. It's very faint, as if it's coming from a long way off, but you can still detect the malicious delight in it. You've obviously chosen the *wrong* colour! You soon find out why. As you breathe in the smoke, you start to choke and splutter: it's poisonous. Clasping a hand to your mouth, you quickly make your way forwards but the smoke is much deeper than it looked. It's as if you're running through an endless fog. You can only hope that you will emerge from it before you have inhaled too much poison. Already, though, you feel yourself weakening . . .

Deduct 1 from your STRENGTH RATING. Go next to 197.

256
THIS CREATURE
IS SLAIN BY

WOUNDS

Wage combat by simultaneously throwing the two dice. If you slay the creature, go to 126. If the creature inflicts a wound on you first, deduct 1 from your STRENGTH RATING and then escape from the pyramid by going to 282.

The creature is at least twice your size, with massive leathery arms.
There are so many sinewy muscles there that the iron armlets round
its biceps look ready to burst. The face is also of tough leather,
almost like the bark of a tree. One would suppose a creature as large

as this wouldn't have need of a weapon. But a weapon it carries; in
the form of a long spear. It tauntingly jabs this spear at the tunnel
wall just behind it to draw your attention to the huge diamond
there.

If you wish to fight creature   **go to 305**
If you wish to avoid it   **go to 281**

258

You step further and further back from the crater so you can give
yourself a good run-up. You allow a ten-metre run . . . then fifteen.
Then, anxiously, you decide you'd better make it twenty. Taking a
deep breath, you charge towards the edge of the crater. As you leap
into the air, you have this terrifying feeling that you're not going to
make it, that you're going to fall short of the other side and drop into

the bottomless darkness. But your feet just touch the crater's opposite lip and, with one desperate effort, you thrust your body forwards on to the hard ground. *Go to 239.*

259

The creature's ferocious roars and howls suddenly fall silent as it doubles up within its cloak and drops to the ground. To your amazement, the cloak then starts to lose its bulk, spilling out across the rocky floor. The creature seems to have dissolved within it! But you have no time to waste in wondering about this. You immediately start to search the cloak for the diamond that you know must be there. Your fingers eventually find it, deep within an inside pocket, and you joyfully transfer it to your haversack.

Add 1 to the score on your TREASURE COUNTER. Now hurry well away from this region by going to 27.

260

Gurn leads you to the far side of the cavern again. You find that it isn't just a solid wall of rock here after all. There's a deep gash hidden behind a large, upright boulder and Gurn squeezes through this. Following him, you find yourself in a partly-lit tunnel. Gurn continues to lead you, making sure you take the correct branch every time the tunnel divides, but eventually he stops. *Go to 73.*

261

Leaving the bread behind you, you only hope that your hours in the mine won't be too many. Your hunger isn't desperate yet but it will surely start to have an effect on your strength *soon*. Of course, Uvane had warned you not to give any of your provisions away, not to be tempted by any of the child beggars you would meet on the way to the mine. You'd thought this very hard of him at the time, but perhaps the Chief Adviser wasn't so unfeeling after all. He probably felt that the best service you could do those children was to make sure that you succeeded in your quest! *Go to 52.*

262

The sword keeps swiping at you, getting closer and closer to finding its target. Using both hands, you frantically swing your shield to the left, then to the right, then to the left again; stumbling behind it. You are very soon exhausted from the incessant onslaught, your arms feeling like lead. It will surely only be a matter of seconds now before the sword finds a way past your sluggish shield . . .

Deduct 1 from your STRENGTH RATING. Go next to 26.

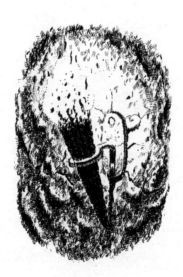

The plant-creature withers immediately you withdraw your sword. Your first blow badly injured it but this second one seems to have struck at its very sap. Just to make sure, though, you keep a watchful eye on those curled-up tendrils as you chip away at the rock surrounding the diamond. You're worried that one of them might suddenly spring to life again and wrap itself round your ankles. But luckily for you the plant-creature remains still . . . and the diamond is now yours.

*Add 1 to the score on your **TREASURE COUNTER**. Now hurry well away from this region by going to 12.*

264

As soon as the goblin has given you the cage, he scurries past into the distant shadows. This makes you wonder whether it *is* some sort of trap. But perhaps the goblin's haste is simply because he wants to reach the safer part of the tunnel, where there's less risk of explosion. You therefore dismiss your suspicions and continue your journey along the tunnel. You're relieved to see that the canary keeps chirping merrily, showing no signs of expiring. But then the chirping suddenly stops . . . ***Go to 138.***

265

A few minutes later another strange occurrence takes place behind this door. Your sword suddenly jumps from your hand and rises into the air. It rises higher and higher, floating towards the tunnel roof way above you. Then it starts to descend slowly again. But it descends not as one sword but as three and they have a strange luminous glow. One glows red, one pure white and one blue. As they come to rest on the ground, you notice that each is engraved with the same cipher: ✳. This is surely telling you which of the three swords you should return to your sheath.

If you have picked up the BOOK OF CIPHERS during your adventure, you may consult it here to find out which of the three swords you should pick up. If not, you'll have to hope for the best in making your decision.

If you choose red sword   **go to 113**
If you choose white sword   **go to 227**
If you choose blue sword   **go to 156**

266

A few moments after the carved pole has disappeared, you hear a sniggering behind you. There's a gnome standing there. He has a long, thin beard and his head is shrouded in a velvet hood. You're just wondering where he came from when you're given something much stranger to wonder at. The gnome suddenly separates into three. One gnome steps out of the original to the left, and another to the right. They then form a close circle round you, joining hands . . . *Go to 93.*

267

You know that it seems mad to head straight for the centre of the whirlwind. But you've come to the conclusion that Murgle is also mad. So perhaps it would be unwise to try and follow logic in dealing with his traps. Unfortunately, though, you've tried to be *too* clever, for as you enter the centre of the whirlwind, it tosses you round furiously. It then swirls your helpless body towards the side of the tunnel, repeatedly dashing it against the rocky wall. Are you strong enough to survive this terrible battering?

Deduct 1 from your STRENGTH RATING. Go next to 307.

268

As soon as this creature's snoring starts to fade behind you, it is replaced by the snoring of another a short distance ahead. This is much louder, suggesting an even larger monster. Turning a bend, you have confirmation of this. The monster is almost *twice as large*, in fact – but so is the magnificent diamond sparkling just above the snoring, bull-like fiend. You're so dazzled by the jewel that you

momentarily forget about the wailing that protects it and reach out to touch its glistening surface. You stop yourself just in time! Then a thought suddenly occurs to you. Why don't you strike the creature *first*? *Now* – while it is still asleep? But as you raise your sword above the snoring fiend, its eyelids flicker and you find that you can't do it. Your conscience won't allow you to kill in cold blood. Even a creature as hideous as this. No, you would insist on waking it first. But dare you? . . .

If you wish to fight creature	**go to 200**
If you wish to avoid it	**go to 29**

269

Her form has separated into three! There are now *three* gowned figures standing there, all identical except for the colour of those gowns. In the middle is still the white-gowned spirit but to her left is a duplicate in green and to her right a duplicate in yellow. Apart from this colour, these vestments are exactly the same; even to identical folds and creases. And they each have the same strange symbol embroidered at their centre . . . *Go to 187.*

270
THIS CREATURE
IS SLAIN BY

WOUNDS

Wage combat by simultaneously throwing the two dice. If you slay the creature, go to 87. If the creature inflicts a wound on you first, deduct 1 from your STRENGTH RATING and then flee well away from this region by hurrying to 5.

Finally, however, the sword drops from your hand, clanking to the ground. Exhausted, you slump back against the tunnel wall. You at last reopen your eyes and, when you do, you notice that the sword has completely lost its red glow. In fact, it looks just like your trusty old friend again. As you bend down to pick it up, however, you're still a little hesitant. Perhaps it will suddenly be possessed by those terrible vibrations again. Your fears prove unjustified, though, and you happily return it to its sheath. *Go to 197.*

272

While you are lying there on the tunnel floor, your dazed mind becomes aware of what seems like fierce fork lightning. Painfully raising your head, you see that it *is* fork lightning. Just a few metres further down the tunnel, zig-zags of blinding light shoot down from the roof. They always come in threes: a fork to the left side of the tunnel, a fork to the right and one striking down the very centre. You seem to hear a voice accompanying the fierce flashes . . . *Go to 131.*

The creature's 'body' proved much tougher than it appeared. But, finally, it drops to the ground. As the abomination writhes about there, yellow liquid starts to ooze from its exposed entrails. The cave is filled with a noxious odour. You work very quickly in extracting the diamond, holding your breath as you chip the rock. The moment the sparkling stone is safely in your haversack, you dash out of the cave. The creature now lies completely still but, just to be on the safe side, you turn the winch again to lower the portcullis.

Add 1 to the score on your TREASURE COUNTER. Go next to 29.

Miraculously, the rock-fall doesn't kill you. But there's a huge boulder lying across your chest and you're much too weak to push it off. Your breathing becomes shorter and shorter, more and more of an effort. Just when you think that it's all over for you, however, you feel your chest lift as the boulder is rolled off your body. Slowly lifting your aching head, you see that there's *another* miner standing over you. You soon discover that this one is very different from the other three, though. For as he offers you his hand to help you to your feet, you realise that you can see right through him . . . *Go to 196.*

275

Luckily, your fingers just manage to grab the edge of the hole in time. But your grip isn't nearly strong enough for you to be able to haul yourself out again. One slight movement and you would drop right down the hole. In fact it looks as if that is to be your fate anyway. The strain on your fingers is immense and you feel their grip loosening. Any moment now, your aching hands are going to have to let go . . .

Deduct 1 from your STRENGTH RATING. Go next to 322.

276

The creature roars after you, furiously banging its head against the portcullis, as you ignore the winch and continue down the tunnel. You very soon come across another monster, though. This one also dwells in a large cave in the tunnel wall and it, too, is restrained by a heavy portcullis. It is rather more passive than the other one, though. Sitting quietly in the shadows at the back of the cave, it watches you with sly, luminous eyes. But you don't allow yourself to be deceived by this passivity. The creature's right claw is restless

on the hilt of a long curved sword. And a blood-thirsty smile grows on its evil face as it moves forward and sees you suddenly spot the huge diamond in its cave . . .

If you wish to fight creature   **go to 58**
If you wish to avoid it   **go to 183**

277

You twist to left and right down this tunnel, following the dim, snaking glow of the lamps. Suddenly, you spot the sparkle of a huge diamond ahead. It's set in the left wall of the tunnel, about a metre from the ground. But there's something standing to the side of this diamond. You can just make out a bulky figure there. As you tensely step nearer this figure, you see that it has the grotesque profile of a monster. Strangely, though, it doesn't make a sound, not even the slightest groan. Wondering if it might be dead, you approach even closer . . . *Go to 125.*

You drop at least five or six metres down the hole but your fingertips just manage to secure enough of a grip on the rock to stop you falling any further. You're left desperately hanging there, knowing that if you let go you will surely be gone for ever. The pothole is clearly very deep. You now try to work your way back up towards the top but the strain on your arms and fingers is immense. They have to support the weight of your whole body since you cannot raise your knees high enough to wedge yourself in the hole. You pray that your poor fingers can hold out long enough . . .

Deduct 1 from your STRENGTH RATING. Go next to 95.

279

Grasping the spirit's right hand, you feel an icy shiver travel right up your arm. It's the coldest flesh you've ever touched, colder than frost. But the surge of cold through your veins suddenly turns to a surge of heat. Your body starts to feel strong again, your head clear. You are about to thank the spirit, but then you notice that she is melting. Soon there is but a pool of water where she stood. In giving *you* strength, had she lost it *herself*? Had the warmth of your hand destroyed her? You prefer not to think about these possibilities, however, and immediately cross over to one of the other cages. You're soon ascending the shaft again.

Add 1 to your STRENGTH RATING. Go next to 247.

'Well, what have we here?' the goblin on the right asks the goblin on the left. 'It looks like a warrior,' answers the other. 'Shall we have some sport with him?' asks the first. 'Why not?' replies the second with a snigger. Both their heads then turn directly towards you and they speak in unison. 'One of us always tells the truth, and one of us always lies. You must guess which of us lies. If you get it wrong you must pay a penalty.'

If you have been taught the TRANCE SPELL during your adventure, you may cast it here to hypnotise the goblins into revealing which is the liar. To do this, place the TRANCE SPELL CARD exactly over their 'mind square' below. If you haven't been taught the TRANCE SPELL, you'll have to hope for the best in making your decision.

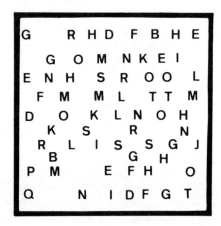

If you think it's goblin on left   **go to 124**
If you think it's goblin on right   **go to 85**

281

You have hurried a good half mile from where you encountered the monster when you hear that strange, squealing laughter again. This time a face *does* appear: a manic, luminous one floating high above you. The hair is long and wild, the green eyes piercing. You were right in thinking that this was the laughter of an old man; the face is at least a hundred years old. 'So you have survived all my monsters and traps!' the apparition sneers and cackles. 'Yes, it is I – Murgle! Draxun's sorcerer!' *Go to 214.*

282

The exit from the mine is only another hundred metres from the pyramid. Your eyes are momentarily dazzled as you emerge into the bright sunshine there. You've done it! You've survived all Murgle's evil creations! But, of course, there was a much more important side to your quest. Your mission wasn't just to survive the mine but also to retrieve as many diamonds as possible. Queen Tarsha and her impoverished kingdom will give you little thanks if you return to her court empty-handed. Only if you can count at least *six* diamonds in your haversack can you truly say that you are the kingdom's saviour.

You have successfully reached the end of the adventure. If you think you could still improve on your performance and collect even more treasures, however, start the game again from paragraph one.

283
THIS CREATURE
IS SLAIN BY

WOUNDS

Wage combat by simultaneously throwing the two dice. If you slay the creature, go to 98. If the creature inflicts a wound on you first, deduct 1 from your STRENGTH RATING and then flee well away from this region by hurrying to 27.

284
You realise that your route is now downwards, for there's a huge, squarish hole in the floor of the cavern. Set into the north and south sides of this hole are series of iron rungs. These two series of rungs were obviously the means by which the mineworkers descended into the hole, and you prepare to climb down one side yourself. Which will you choose?

If you have acquired the POWER OF FORESIGHT during your adventure so far, you may employ it here to find out whether you should avoid one series of rungs. To do this, place the FORESIGHT POWER CARD exactly over the 'eye' shape below. If you haven't acquired FORESIGHT POWER, you'll have to hope for the best in making your decision.

If you choose rungs on north side   **go to 6**
If you choose rungs on south side   **go to 251**

285

You reluctantly leave the diamond behind, afraid to bring the creature to life. You couldn't be sure that it wouldn't have proved far too strong an opponent. There was no way of telling how agile the creature might be, how fierce. But you have the same problem again when you turn the next bend in the tunnel. For there's another fabulous diamond there . . . and another frozen creature standing beside it. As soon as you move your hand up to the diamond, the creature's hideous nostrils start to flare. And its claw

twitches on the battle-axe it holds. Clearly, this creature too will immediately come to life should you try and remove the diamond . . .

If you wish to fight creature   **go to 62**
If you wish to avoid it   **go to 303**

286

You put the thick iron helmet on your head, guessing that the danger spoken of by the wizard is most likely to be a rock-fall. You now cautiously proceed along the tunnel. Suddenly your ears are assaulted by a piercing wail. It seems to penetrate straight to your brain and you clamp your hands to your ears in a desperate attempt to block it out. But it's to no avail. You quickly grow dizzy from the excruciating sound and collapse to the ground. If it doesn't stop soon, then it will surely be the end of you . . .

Deduct 1 from your STRENGTH RATING. Go next to 15.

287

You hurry the few paces to the other side of the crater, and start to scramble up towards the top again. You're about two-thirds of the way there, however, when you suddenly feel a searing pain in your hand. Something has bitten you – a poisonous grub of some sort, living in the rock's cracks. Its poison works quickly because your arm soon starts to feel very weak. You only hope that the poison is not deadly – and that you can hold out until you reach the top of the crater. If you fell now, from this height, you probably wouldn't survive!

Deduct 1 from your STRENGTH RATING. Go next to 107.

288

At last the creature falls from your sword-strikes. It was even more resilient than you'd expected and after all your exertions you drop to the ground yourself! But then you catch sight of the diamond again and its glinting magnificence quickly inspires you to get on your feet again.

Add 1 to the score on your TREASURE COUNTER. Now hurry well away from this region by going to 27.

The seemingly endless tunnel that leads away from the cavern gradually becomes narrower and narrower, its roof lower and lower. The flickering glow from the lamps now bathes the entire width. The glares flicker right across the roof, spilling in and out of the cracks and crevices, and dance down the opposite walls. But then the tunnel starts to widen again and the reach of the glow shortens. The light is quickly consumed by dark shadows once more. This much wider tunnel eventually divides into two smaller ones, though; one branching off to the left and one to the right. Which one will you follow?

If you have acquired the power of FORESIGHT, you may employ it here to find out if either of the tunnels should be avoided. To do this, place the FORESIGHT POWER CARD exactly over the 'eye' shape below. If you haven't acquired the power of FORESIGHT, you'll have to hope for the best in making your choice.

If you choose left   **go to 150**
If you choose right   **go to 45**

'Oh, how easily deceived you are!' the mysterious laughter booms. 'That is just "fool's diamond". It might have the likeness of a diamond but it's merely a piece of worthless rock. Do you think that it would have been left so unprotected otherwise?' You are so angry with this mocking faceless voice that you immediately hurl the rock in the direction from which it seems to originate. This only serves to anger the voice as well, however, and the 'diamond' causes a large explosion as it hits the ground. A piece of flying debris strikes your forehead, badly gashing it.

Deduct 1 from your STRENGTH RATING. Go next to 221.

291
THIS CREATURE
IS SLAIN BY

WOUNDS

Wage combat by simultaneously throwing the two dice. If you slay the creature, go to 219. If the creature inflicts a wound on you first, deduct 1 from your STRENGTH RATING and then flee well away from this region by hurrying to 12.

You watch, horrified, as the creature drags its fatally-wounded body across the hard ground. It's heading for the ravine and the wall of fire burning within it! It obviously wants to put an end to itself immediately rather than suffer a slow, writhing death. You can watch no more, turning your eyes instead to the diamond in the tunnel wall. As you chip it out, you expect at every second to hear the creature's plunging scream behind you. But there's just silence. Even so, when you finally look back towards the wall of fire, the fiend is no more.

Add 1 to the score on your TREASURE COUNTER. Now hurry well away from this region by going to 12.

293

The bedevilled shovel now wraps itself round your calves, spiralling further and further up your body. You quickly reach for your sword to hack it off but the shovel is at your waist before you can draw it. You lie there helpless as the shovel now moves up to your chest, starting to constrict it. It squeezes harder and harder. Only some while after you have passed out does it convert to the innocent shovel again and drop to the ground. Is there just enough strength left in you to start breathing again?

Deduct 1 from your STRENGTH RATING. Go next to 198.

294

The creature is as grotesque as the diamond is beautiful. A huge, lumpy head rests snarling on a muscular body. The snarl is a mixture of fangs and small tusks, and two deep-set eyes glare with evil above them. Grasped in the fiend's hand is a razor-sharp sword.

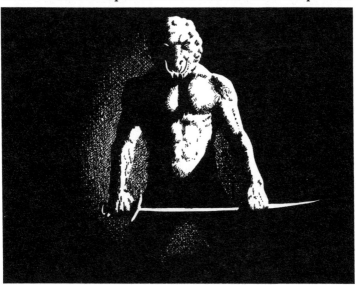

You realise that if you are going to make that diamond your own, you are going to have to challenge this horrendous creature.

If you wish to fight creature **go to 16**
If you wish to avoid it **go to 147**

295

Your conscience is now clear! Although the combat was close and terrifying, the diamond is now yours and those starving urchins can be fed. You use the dead creature's axe to hack the massive gem free from the surrounding rock. You then carefully place it in your haversack, knowing how many thousands of hearts it can cheer.

Add 1 to the score on your TREASURE COUNTER. Now hurry well away from this region by going to 12.

Keeping as close as you can to the left side of the tunnel, you suddenly rub against a strange lichen growing on the wall. It leaves a purplish dust on your arm and shoulder. You try to brush this dust off but it seems to adhere like a scab. You become alarmed as you feel the strength suddenly draining from your arm and then from that whole side of your body. You quickly move across to the other wall, rubbing the infested arm against the rough rock there. It's absolute agony but you know that you must scrape the lichen right off if you're going to survive . . .

Deduct 1 from your STRENGTH RATING. Go next to 328.

297

As you are walking along the right side of the tunnel, keeping as close to the wall as possible, you suddenly become aware of a sharp pain in your arm. Several sharp pains, in fact, running from your wrist right up to your shoulder. Anxiously glancing down, you see that there are a mass of tiny spikes sticking into your flesh. They've rubbed off from an evil-looking cactus-like plant growing on the rock. They must be tipped with poison because you feel yourself rapidly growing weak. You frantically start to pull the spikes out but will you be able to remove them all in time?

Deduct 1 from your STRENGTH RATING. Go next to 221.

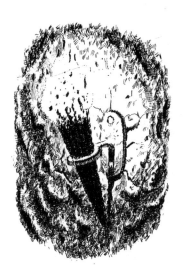

298

At last you reach the bottom of the huge pole again, bending down to pick up your sword. You are returning the weapon to its sheath at your waist when a goblin appears in front of you. This is no ordinary goblin, though. His flesh keeps changing colour: one moment it is red, the next green . . . and the next it is a fluorescent yellow. You again wonder whether your imagination is playing tricks on you, but then the strange creature starts to speak. *Go to 232.*

299

You lean on your sword, resting a while before going over to the diamond. You're quite exhausted from that prolonged and bloody conflict. Besides, you want to make sure that the creature is completely dead before you turn your back on it. Although its body lies perfectly still, some of the maggots continue to writhe on its scalp. But their number diminishes and eventually every one of them is still as well. You can now safely give your attention to the diamond.

Add 1 to the score on your TREASURE COUNTER. Now hurry well away from this region by going to 281.

300
THIS CREATURE
IS SLAIN BY

WOUNDS

Wage combat by simultaneously throwing the two dice. If you slay the creature, go to 53. If the creature inflicts a wound on you first, deduct 1 from your STRENGTH RATING and then flee well away from this region by hurrying to 12.

301
You haven't walked much further along the tunnel when it suddenly broadens out into a huge cavern. The miners had obviously worked hard here, for there is a multitude of caves hacked into its sides. You therefore assume that this is an area particularly rich in diamonds. You immediately spot confirmation of this – for there's a brilliant gleam from the nearest cave. Lying atop a heap of fallen rocks on the cave floor is a magnificent, sparkling diamond. But this is not all that gleams in the shadows of that cave . . . ***Go to 28.***

Clasping the double's hand, you're surprised at how light it is. Your own hand seems to go right through it as though it's hardly there. The magic in it, though, is very strong. You immediately feel a surge of power pass from the double's hand to your own. It runs all the way up your arm and into the rest of your body. Invigorated, you rise to your feet. You're just about to thank the double, however, when he vanishes into thin air. Again, you start to wonder if this was all just an illusion.

Add 1 to your STRENGTH RATING. Go next to 197.

303

Another bend in the tunnel leads to a third diamond and a third grotesque creature. It's little surprise to you now that the fiend stands there completely frozen. Completely frozen that is until you

move your hand towards the diamond. Then, like the previous two, the creature starts to show signs of life. Its leathery eyelids flicker. Its tusked mouth starts to drool. Again, its weapon twitches in its grasp. On this occasion the weapon is a huge mace. Proof that the mace has already seen action is evident from the dried blood and tufts of hair on its cruel spikes. How do you rate your own chances against it?

> If you wish to fight creature   **go to 175**
> If you wish to avoid it   **go to 164**

304

You stab your sword into the middle bubble, although careful not to thrust too far in case you injure the double trapped inside. You were hoping that the whole thing would disappear once you had popped it but you have to slice the bubble right open, from top to bottom. At last the cut is wide enough for the double to step through. All your efforts were for nothing, though, because the double suddenly vanishes into thin air. It was just an illusion. At least this bubble wasn't any sort of trap, though. *Go to 265.*

305
THIS CREATURE
IS SLAIN BY

WOUNDS

Wage combat by simultaneously throwing the two dice. If you slay the creature, go to 59. If the creature inflicts a wound on you first, deduct 1 from your STRENGTH RATING and then flee well away from this region by hurrying to 281.

306

You desperately call to Lekk to help you out of the hole. As he approaches above you, however, you notice that he is smiling. You realise from that ghastly smile that he is a traitor miner . . . that he must be secretly working for Murgle. The smile broadens as he lifts one of his iron-studded boots and grinds it on your fingers. You shriek in agony. It's not just the pain that makes you shriek, though. It's the knowledge that at any second now your hands will have to let go . . .

Deduct 1 from your STRENGTH RATING. Go next to 163.

307

At last the whirlwind slows down, finally stopping altogether. It was only just in time because your battered body couldn't have taken a second more. You lie there, exhausted, on the hard ground, waiting until your brain stops spinning as well. Then you rise shakily to your feet. You wonder what other nightmares are in store for you behind this door. *Go to 197.*

You watch the unpleasant creature's face as you slowly take the phial of yellow potion from him. It's still grinning maliciously, but you can't work out whether that's because you have made the wrong choice or simply because it's enjoying your agonised hesitation. You decide that if it's the latter you won't give him that pleasure for a second longer. So you immediately remove the cork and put the phial to your lips. *Go to 94.*

You pick up the middle goblet and raise it to your lips. You can't actually see any potion in there at all. There's just the swirling vapour which seems to go all the way to the bottom. The vapour doesn't appear harmful in any way, though. It's not scalding hot, like it looks. Nor does it have a noxious smell. So you start to swallow it as if it were a liquid. Immediately you have emptied the goblet, your dazed head clears and all your aches and bruises disappear. You are now ready to continue along this escape route to the outside.

Add 1 to your STRENGTH RATING. Go next to 123.

310

Gurn tells you there is another route in and out of the mine, besides the one that you took. 'It is in fact a far quicker way to the outside,' he adds, 'but it emerges a good three or four miles from the village and so was only used as an escape route in case of falls or floods in the main tunnels. Come, one of us will be your guide. Choose who you will.'

If you choose Gurn himself	**go to 260**
If you choose Lekk	**go to 31**
If you choose Nabel	**go to 158**

311

You find the monster just round the next bend, slumped directly beneath one of the flickering lamps. Even in sleep it is quite grotesque – perhaps even more so. Its snores gurgle in a gaping red throat. Trapped between its fang-like teeth are morsels of un-digested flesh and you shudder to think where this came from. A fortune-hunter like yourself? But you put such macabre thoughts aside and stealthily reach for the diamond just above the fiend. It looks quite loose in the rock. Your fingers are about to touch it,

however, when a piercing wail rings out through the tunnel. The creature starts to wake so you quickly withdraw your hand and the wail suddenly stops again. Removing that diamond is not going to be as easy as you thought! Murgle has obviously protected it with a magic alarm so that you have to fight the creature first . . .

If you wish to fight creature   **go to 189**
If you wish to avoid it   **go to 88**

312

The cage hasn't climbed much further up the shaft when a small hole appears in the corner of the floor opposite you. It seems as if something is eating away at it because it quickly grows bigger. Within seconds the whole of the right side of the floor has disappeared. You edge back, right against the wooden bars of the cage, worried that the hole will now spread across to your side.

Fortunately, however, this is as large as it gets. As long as you are careful where you put your feet, the gaping hole shouldn't pose any danger. **Go to 247.**

313
THIS CREATURE
IS SLAIN BY

WOUNDS

Wage combat by simultaneously throwing the two dice. If you slay the creature, go to 82. If the creature inflicts a wound on you first, deduct 1 from your STRENGTH RATING and then flee well away from this region by hurrying to 29.

314
'I'm a miner,' the man explains when he sees that you are no more than a human being yourself. 'At least, I *was* a miner. For the last few years, I've been a hermit, hiding from Draxun's monsters. That's why I have *three* ropes dangling from my cave. Only one is safe – for the few occasions I have to venture out from my cave to look for food. The other two are traps for any monsters that might come sniffing round this way. You were lucky to chose the correct rope!' **Go to 171.**

Stepping through the door on the left, you find yourself looking up at a huge statue. It's of a seated goddess which seems at least ten times your height. It can't be, though, because this part of the tunnel is at most five metres high! This incongruity is very soon forgotten, though, for you suddenly notice a massive diamond set into the goddess's forehead. You're just about to start climbing the statue when you notice a cryptic inscription carved into the statue's feet: **XYXYXYX**. You hesitate for a moment, wondering whether this is warning you against trying to climb for the diamond.

If you have picked up the CRYPTICS SCROLL during your adventure, you may consult it here to find out the meaning of the inscription. If you haven't, you'll have to hope for the best in making your decision.

If you decide to climb statue   **go to 191**
If you decide to ignore it   **go to 230**

316

There's a blood-curdling howl from the creature as it staggers backwards. It desperately tries to staunch its many wounds – shifting its clawed hands from one to the other, pressing them hard – but it's quite hopeless. The life is fast draining away from the monster. It's now on its knees, now writhing on the rocky floor. When its twitchings have at last ceased, you step over the grotesque body towards the back of the cave. You chip at the rock there with your sword, working it all the way round the diamond. Fortunately, the rock here is quite soft and the jewel is soon freed. You hold it up to the nearest lamp, again admiring its beauty, before placing it into your haversack.

Add 1 to the score on your TREASURE COUNTER. Now hurry well away from this region by going to 5.

317

At last the sucking fungi release you but you collapse weak and dizzy to the ground. 'Oh, foolish one!' speaks the white-gowned spirit, looking down on you. Her face is now a blackened skull. 'Foolish to think that Murgle would make it so easy for you!' she adds. 'Because I appeared to you first doesn't mean that I am the original guardian spirit. No, I am one of her evil clones! But not so evil as the other clone, not so evil that I won't give you a chance to restore the strength that the fungi have sucked from you.' *Go to 65.*

318

The sorcerer explains that he was Murgle's predecessor at Draxun's court but was ousted by Murgle. 'If I hadn't fled,' his deep, echoing voice tells you, 'if I hadn't hidden myself deep down here, that evil usurper would have killed me. But I shall have my revenge! Part of my revenge will be by helping you. But that can only be done if you also help yourself . . .' The sorcerer suddenly extends his arm and, to your amazement, three hooded robes magically appear, draped over it. One is of wool, one of velvet and one of silk. 'If you wrap yourself in the right robe,' he tells you, 'then the secret of one of my spells will immediately be yours.'

If you choose woollen robe	**go to 8**
If you choose velvet robe	**go to 205**
If you choose silk robe	**go to 139**

319

Perhaps you were right to leave that diamond behind because you soon come across an even larger one. But the creature that snarls in front of it is also much larger. Despite its hunched stance, it must be

at least a metre taller than you. Its huge, ape-like face flickers with ugly, red shadows as it too tries to keep as far away from the flames as possible. There's the same flickering red reflected in the blade of its weapon – a hefty double-headed axe. You're sure you wouldn't stand a chance against this monster, for there's also spiked armour protecting large areas of its body. So you again keep as close to the wall of fire as possible, edging past the fiend. But then your gaze guiltily returns to that massive diamond in the rock behind it. The gold it would fetch would surely be enough to feed every single starving child in this kingdom . . .

If you wish to fight creature **go to 140**
If you wish to avoid it **go to 220**

320

'You chose wrongly!' the old hag says, cackling and revealing a black-toothed grin. Still cackling, she then starts to walk away from you, into the shadows. 'Nidir!' you desperately shout after her. And then, 'Kadris!' But she refuses to respond to either name, suddenly merging with the darkness. As she had warned, she has only allowed you one chance! But your eyes can focus properly now and you've recovered enough from the effects of the slime to be able to rise to your feet. You certainly don't feel as strong as you were before – but at least there still seems to be enough stamina in you for you to continue with your quest. *Go to 4.*

321

As it drops to the ground, howling and screaming, the creature becomes an even uglier sight. Those cavernous black and red shadows now writhe right across its face, the darkness penetrating deep into its gaping throat. That throat rasps and gurgles as the warty limbs quiver against the hard rock. Finally, though, it is still and you immediately turn your attention to the diamond. When you have prised it from the rock, you allow yourself a few seconds to admire its beauty. You turn the stone slowly, making the imprisoned reflections flame within it. But then you carefully put the diamond away in your haversack. Its beauty is nothing compared to the good it can provide.

Add 1 to the score on your TREASURE COUNTER. Now hurry well away from this region by going to 12.

322

Suddenly you feel someone grab hold of your two wrists. It's Nabel! He then heaves you out of the hole. 'You were meant to be following me,' he scolds you. 'It took me a while to find you. Why did you wander down this branch? It's full of danger.' But then he sees your searching frown as you try to work out which of the two Nabels this is. 'Ah, so that's what happened!' He nods knowingly as he leads you back to the other branch of the tunnel. 'You followed a mirage of me. That would be Murgle up to his evil magic again. Perhaps, to be on the safe side, I should take my leave of you here. Anyway, your path is direct from now on.' ***Go to 123.***

323

It's not long before you encounter yet another creature in this part of the tunnel. Again, you carefully skirt it while you weigh up your chances. It's the strangest monster you've seen yet, more like a moving plant than a beast. The head is a fungus and the limbs woody tendrils. The whole thing is infested with aphids and beetles. Suddenly one of the tendrils lashes out at you, and you realise that these are what you must be most wary of if you decide to

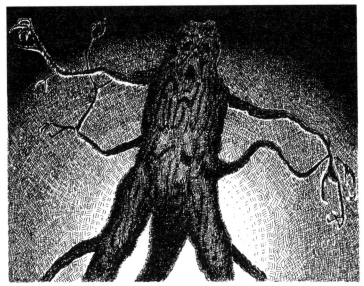

fight it. The tendril hits the ground with the force of a felled tree! Still unsure whether to fight it or not, you try to spot the diamond it protects in the tunnel wall behind it. Perhaps *that* will help you make up your mind. Ah, there it is! Probably the finest specimen you've yet seen in the mine . . .

If you wish to fight creature	**go to 36**
If you wish to avoid it	**go to 12**

324

After you have tossed the bottom pebble out of the cage, you wait to see what happens next. For a moment nothing, but then the remaining pebble starts to grow. It grows bigger and bigger and you desperately heave on the rope to stop the cage descending from all this extra weight. At last it stops but the pebble is now the size of a small boulder. The cage's progress up the shaft is now only fraction by fraction and your muscles quickly tire from this strenuous work. You know that you daren't let go of the rope, though. If you do, both you and the cage will plummet to the bottom of the shaft . . .

Deduct 1 from your STRENGTH RATING. Go next to 247.

325

As you continue to heave on the rope, making the cage slowly climb higher and higher, you wonder how much further there is to go. Twenty metres? Fifty? A hundred? You also wonder whether the top of the shaft will soon bring you to the exit from the mine. You can't wait to see daylight again, to breathe fresh air. This dark, claustrophobic, hideous place is finally becoming too much for you. **Go to 169.**

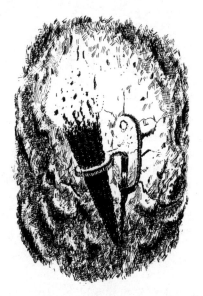

326

'My name is Oblad, slave of this lamp,' the figure tells you. 'The palm of one of my hands has been branded with a cross to denote my slavery. If you can tell me *which* palm, then your path will continue to be illuminated by the lamps. But if your answer is wrong, the next thirty lamps will immediately extinguish and you will be in total darkness. So choose well, my friend. Is the brand hidden in my left palm or my right?'

If you have been taught the TRANCE SPELL during your adventure, you may cast it here to hypnotise the slave into telling you which palm contains the brand. To do this, place the TRANCE SPELL CARD exactly over the slave's 'mind square' below. If you haven't been taught the TRANCE SPELL, you'll have to hope for the best in making your decision.

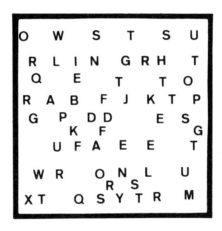

If you choose his left palm   **go to 61**
If you choose his right palm   **go to 102**

327

The spirit's left hand pulls you to your feet but it seems to do little more than that. You feel just as weak as you were before. You now wonder whether you should make a grab at the spirit's other hand but she suddenly starts to melt! A few moments later, she is just a pool of water on the ground. You are stunned by this but you quickly gather your wits again. You cross over to one of the other cages and step inside. You still have just enough strength to make the cage slowly take you up the shaft once more. *Go to 247.*

328

This branch of the tunnel eventually merges with the other two again and it's once more a small cavern that you're walking through. You jump as you suddenly hear squealing laughter from the darkness ahead. It sounds as if it belongs to a manic old man but you're unable to see any face there. As the laughter fades away it is replaced by a very different sound; one which concerns you even more . . . *Go to 238.*

329
THIS CREATURE
IS SLAIN BY

WOUNDS

Wage combat by simultaneously throwing the two dice. If you slay the creature, go to 126. If the creature inflicts a wound on you first, deduct 1 from your STRENGTH RATING and then escape from the pyramid by going to 282.

330

The apparition seems to be the spectre of one of the former mineworkers for it carries the vague form of a pickaxe over its transparent shoulder. Suddenly it beckons you with a white, wispy finger. You quickly turn away from it, about to flee back in the direction you came from, but to your horror you notice another apparition hovering behind you. This one also seems to be the spectre of a past miner . . . and it too is beckoning you. You're clearly going to have to approach one of them. But which?

| If spectre in front | **go to 137** |
| If spectre behind | **go to 212** |